DANIEL COLTON KIDNAPPED

ELAINE SCHULTE

BJU PRESS
Greenville, South Carolina

Library of Congress Cataloging-in-Publication Data
Schulte, Elaine L.
  Daniel Colton kidnapped / Elaine Schulte.
     p. cm. — (Colton cousins adventure ; bk. 4)
  Summary: In the late 1840s, having been led by God to an old Spanish
ranch outside San Francisco, thirteen-year-old Daniel and his cousin
Suzannah see their dream of a permanent home threatened by the
moneymaking schemes of the evil Charles Herrington.
  ISBN 1-57924-566-8 (alk. paper)
  [1. Frontier and pioneer life—California—Fiction. 2. San Francisco
(Calif.)—Fiction. 3. Christian life—Fiction.] I. Title.
PZ7.S3867 Dak 2002
  [Fic]—dc21

                                                         2001007884

Daniel Colton Kidnapped

Elaine Schulte

Designed by Jamie Leong
Cover and illustrations by Johanna Berg Ehnis

©1993 Elaine Schulte
©2002 Bob Jones University Press
Greenville, SC 29614

ISBN 1-57924-566-8

15 14 13 12 11 10 9 8 7 6 5 4 3 2 1

To the shining lights at ECS
on Idaho Avenue in Escondido

COLTON COUSINS ADVENTURE SERIES

Suzannah and the Secret Coins
Daniel Colton Under Fire
Suzannah Strikes Gold
Daniel Colton Kidnapped

CONTENTS

Chapter 1 1

Chapter 2 13

Chapter 3 25

Chapter 4 36

Chapter 5 49

Chapter 6 71

Chapter 7 82

Chapter 8 92

Chapter 9 103

Chapter 10 117

Epilogue 136

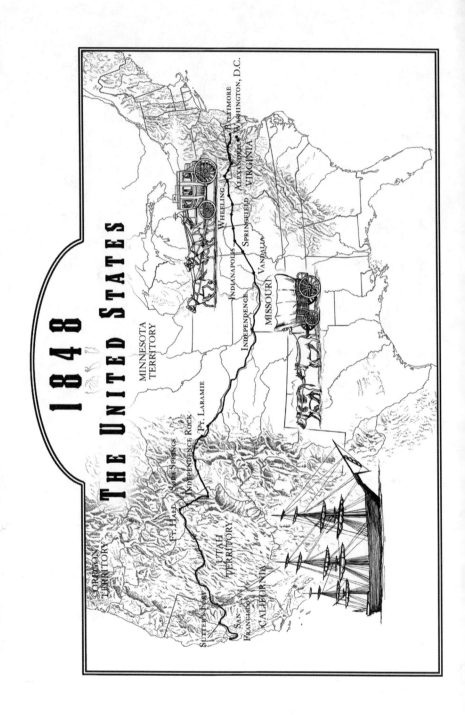

1848

THE UNITED STATES

OREGON TERRITORY

MINNESOTA TERRITORY

UTAH TERRITORY

CALIFORNIA

MISSOURI

VIRGINIA

WASHINGTON, D.C.

BALTIMORE

ALEXANDRIA

WHEELING

SPRINGFIELD

VANDALIA

INDIANAPOLIS

INDEPENDENCE

FT. LARAMIE

INDEPENDENCE ROCK

SODA SPRINGS

FT. HALL

SUTTER'S FORT

SAN FRANCISCO

Daniel Colton felt the hair on the back of his neck stand straight up. *Was that a face peering out the window of the house up ahead?*

He looked harder.

No one at the window now. Probably it had been his imagination, since he could barely see through the gray December drizzle.

Trudging beside the four oxen pulling his family's covered wagon, Daniel shouted, "Giddap! We're almost to Rancho Encino, our new home!"

The last hundred miles had seemed the longest since the wagon train left Independence, Missouri nearly eight months ago. Through barren desert and jutting mountains they had pushed steadily westward, stopping only for a few months in the gold fields. Now that he was in sight of the California hacienda his father had bought, Daniel was eager for their long trek to end.

As the two wagons belonging to the Colton family pulled nearer the sprawling ranch, he glanced around. A large adobe house stood in the midst of graceful pepper trees, its whitewashed walls bright even in the drizzle. Everything looked peaceful enough. No horses in sight—not at the hitching post, not in the corral. No smoke curling from the chimney either, though he thought he'd seen traces of it earlier.

"Giddap!" he shouted at the oxen again. "We're almost there!"

Suzannah, his twelve-year-old cousin, poked her head out of the front flap of the wagon, her blue-green eyes wide. "Never expected such a big house," she said. "Not after those teensy little cabins in the gold hills."

"Father did say there'd be room for all of us. Won't that be something though? All twelve of us living in one house!"

Suzannah rolled her eyes skyward. "Thirteen, if Charles comes to live with us."

Daniel winced. If he never saw Charles Herrington again as long as he lived, it would be too soon to suit him. Cousin Pauline's no-account gambler husband seemed to attract trouble wherever he went. Most likely, he was in nearby San Francisco right now, setting up another gambling tent, while poor Pauline and their two babies bumped along in the wagon.

Ahead, Father drove his oxen and wagon through the gateposts, not that there was a gate, nor even fences, except for the corral by the whitewashed barn.

"Here I come!" Suzannah warned. She gathered up her red calico skirt and jumped down, her braids bobbing against her dark blue cloak. "Come a ways with me," she whispered to Daniel, "I don't want Pauline to hear."

Curious, Daniel hurried to catch up.

As they reached the two lead oxen, she spoke in a low voice. "Do you get the feeling we're being watched?"

He looked again at the bare windows. "Maybe. But it's probably just light reflecting off the glass."

"In this weather?"

Daniel shrugged, hoping she wouldn't press for an answer. He wasn't ready to tell her what he thought he'd seen. He liked to study on a thing, while Suzannah jumped to conclusions.

She gave his shoulder a jab. "Remember back in Bannock Indian territory, when I told you I thought we were being watched? And sure enough, we were! By that Indian girl Garth almost shot!"

For a moment Daniel could almost smell the damp, mossy woods, see the crouching figure on the creek bank, hear the sharp report of his stepcousin's rifle as it went off, just as Daniel lunged to knock the gun out of Garth's hands—

"Daniel Meriwether Colton!" Suzannah said. "Are you listening to me? We may be in danger!"

"If there's someone in the house, it's probably only squatters."

"Squatters?"

"Father says folks are coming from all over, looking for gold, and some of them don't care whose property they move in on."

Suzannah's eyes widened. "Then I'm telling your father what I saw. If someone's in the house, Uncle Franklin needs to know."

She hurried ahead and caught up with the lead wagon. Falling into step beside him, she talked fast, her brown braids bobbing. She watched as Father eyed the house and said something in low tones. Then she turned and started back toward Daniel with a frown.

"What's wrong?" he asked.

"He thinks it's my imagination."

"Here," Daniel said, handing over his whip to Suzannah. "Keep the oxen in line. I have something to say to Father too. It couldn't be both of our imaginations."

Mud clung to his boots as he hurried to his father. If someone were watching from the house, he hoped they couldn't see how scared he was. He hoped all they could see was a freckle-faced thirteen-year-old boy who was excited about reaching his new home, but his heart hammered so loudly he thought the whole California territory could hear it.

As he passed the covered wagon where Mother was riding, her round face smiled out from the arched opening. "Isn't the house charming? And there's a barn and chicken coop too. We'll have eggs again!"

Daniel managed to nod and smile back. But the famous Colton grin faded from his face as soon as he reached his father's side and shared his suspicions.

Father glanced toward the house and drew in a deep breath. "Go to the wagon and load your rifle, Son. Don't make a big show of it. Just do it. And tell Suzannah to tie the oxen to the hitching post."

"What's wrong, Franklin?" Mother called from the wagon. "Is something amiss?"

Father spoke quietly. "Better load my rifle for me, Ruthie. Back in the wagon where no one can see you at it."

Daniel tried not to walk too fast. Best to appear calm.

"Told you!" Suzannah crowed triumphantly when Daniel whispered the instructions to her. "Someone *is* in there."

"Keep quiet, and try not to look scared," he cautioned. Then he wondered why he bothered. Suzannah Elizabeth Colton was not the kind of girl to scare easily. Sometimes it seemed she *looked* for danger!

Daniel climbed onto the driver's seat and into the wagon, closing the canvas flaps behind him. Inside, Suzannah's sister Pauline was resting on the quilts with two-year-old Jamie and the new baby, Annie.

When Daniel took down his rifle from its peg, Pauline sat up in alarm, a few wisps of golden hair curling from her bonnet. "Whatever is wrong?"

He spoke softly so he wouldn't awaken the baby. "Appears someone's in the house."

"Oh, no!" Pauline's skin, brown from the desert sun, faded to pale ivory. "Not again. I hoped everything would be different here."

Jamie looked at the rifle. "Gun," he said. "Gun."

"Rifle," Daniel corrected, and carefully poured in a load of powder.

"Do you think there'll be shooting?"

Daniel shrugged, trying not to think about it. He had hated guns ever since he'd heard about the boy who'd actually killed his own father in a hunting accident back home in Virginia. Daniel had carried a rifle many times, of course. Menfolk had to protect their families and shoot game for food. But he'd never killed anyone. And he didn't want to start today either.

He crawled back out of the wagon, taking care not to reveal the weapon. It was hard, walking with the rifle tucked out of sight under his poncho. It slapped against his leg as he hurried back to his father.

"Maybe they ran out the back when they saw us coming," Daniel told him, hoping with all his might that it was so.

Father looked concerned. "We'll see, Son."

They started toward the house. Just the two of them against who-knew-how-many inside. *Lord, help us,* Daniel prayed. *Help us know what to do*—

"Come on," Father said, "this is our house . . . the house the Lord has provided for us."

They walked up the flagstone path to the arched entryway. At the door, Father's big hand reached for the wrought-iron handle. But before he could touch it, the heavy brown door swung open.

Charles! Charles Herrington!

It was Pauline's husband—tall, dark, and handsome as ever. Dressed in a fine black suit, with a gold watch chain swinging from his vest pocket, he looked just like a riverboat gambler. "Welcome to the hacienda," he said as if he owned the place. "You'll be glad to hear I've been keeping the house warm for you."

Daniel slowly put down his rifle.

"How on earth did you know this was our house?" Father demanded.

"News travels fast in San Francisco," Charles replied with a lofty smile, "especially when someone buys an old Spanish ranch. Appears you did well for yourself in the gold fields."

"No thanks to you!" Daniel blurted. The last time he'd seen Charles, the man had tied Daniel to a bunk bed in their cabin. He'd even tied Pauline—his own wife who was expecting their baby—into a rocking chair! On top of that, he'd tried to steal Suzannah's gold nuggets.

But Charles seemed to be suffering no guilt over any of it. He simply ignored Daniel. "I assume my wife is out in the wagon."

Father's usually kind face was stiff with anger. "She is, though I wouldn't be surprised if she refuses to have anything more to do with you. You could have killed her . . . and your unborn baby too!"

"I knew you'd be along sooner or later," Charles said, as if Father hadn't spoken.

"What kind of man *are* you, to treat your wife like that?" Father asked, outraged.

Charles stared down at his fine leather boots. "I don't suppose you'll forgive me for . . . an error in judgment, would you?"

"An error in judgment?" Father echoed, furious.

Charles jutted out his chin. "I suppose *you're* always perfect?"

Father pressed his lips together as if to guard his tongue. "Only one Man who's ever lived on this earth was perfect, and it certainly wasn't any one of us."

Daniel drew a deep breath. "You could at least have left Lucky in the corral so we'd know it was *you* in the house," he told Charles.

"And risk having him stolen?" Charles stared at Daniel as if he'd lost his mind. "You can't be too careful in California. There are thieves everywhere."

You ought to know, since you're one yourself! Daniel thought, but he kept it to himself.

After a long moment, Father said, "I may forgive you this time, Charles, but I won't forget. If I ever catch you treating my niece badly again—" He let the unspoken threat linger.

"I'll do better," Charles promised, and Daniel guessed that was as close to an apology as Charles Herrington would get.

Father shook his head. "Call the family in."

Daniel stepped back through the gate. "It's only Charles!" he yelled out.

"This way," Father said to the weary travelers as they left the wagons. "Let's go inside."

They scraped the mud from their boots, then walked through the white-walled entrance toward an enclosed courtyard with a fine fountain. The rooms of the house formed a U-shape that opened onto a roofed, red-tiled veranda overlooking the courtyard garden.

Rounding the corner, they headed for the first door. "The parlor," Charles told them as if conducting a tour.

Daniel clamped his lips shut before he said something he'd be sorry for later.

Inside, the parlor walls were whitewashed too, and the timbered ceiling was tied together with strips of rawhide. Heavy dark furniture stood on a bright rug, the only spot of color in the room. The fireplace smelled of wet ashes, as if someone had flung water on the fire when he heard them coming. Was Charles in trouble again? Had he mistaken them for someone else?

When Pauline arrived with the children, she glanced nervously at her husband. Even little Jamie hid behind her skirts. "Hello, Charles," she said, keeping her distance.

He stepped forward and kissed her cheek, making her flinch. "Well, my dear. I see you're looking much more like the girl I married." He eyed her slim figure with admiration. "Now are you going to let me see our new baby?"

Pauline edged toward Father, as if seeking his protection, then bravely held out the baby for Charles's inspection.

Daniel watched as Charles lifted a corner of the blanket. Little Annie blinked her blue eyes at him, sweet as an angel, then suddenly puckered up her face and began to cry fiercely.

"Oh, well," Charles said, withdrawing his hand. "There's plenty of time for us to get acquainted." Then pasting on his brightest smile, he made a little bow. "Shall we sit down?" He offered a horsehair chair to Pauline and another to Mother, who greeted him with suspicion.

They all sat stiffly, not quite knowing what to say. Finally Annie quieted and Charles asked, "Where are the others?"

After another awkward silence, Mother replied, "Pearl and her family will be here in a few days. Ned Taylor and Big Red too."

Daniel was beginning to wonder where Suzannah was when she rushed in, all out of breath. She stopped short when she saw her brother-in-law. "Charles," she said coldly. "Should have known it'd be *you.*"

"Well, if it isn't Suzannah," he said. "Your nose is red."

She shot back, "That's because I've been out in the cold barn with your horse Lucky. He looked so lonesome that I slapped him on his backside and sent him running all the way back to Alexandria, Virginia."

"You did *what?*" Charles jumped up and hurried to the window, followed by Daniel. There was no sign of Charles's chestnut stallion.

Suzannah folded her arms. "I didn't do it, but I should have. After what you did . . . tying down Pauline and Daniel, and taking my gold nuggets."

"Suzannah." Mother warned. Looking around, Daniel saw that the whole family was tense.

Suzannah lifted her chin and made a face at Charles. Daniel couldn't blame her. She'd been through a lot since her parents—and Pauline's—had died in a steamboat explosion back in Virginia. Right after that, Pauline had married Charles, probably hoping he'd take care of them. Instead, he'd made their lives even more miserable with his gambling and drinking and running out on them.

Just then Annie began to scream again. Charles turned to Pauline. "Why don't you do something?" he said roughly. "You know how I dislike squalling babies."

Mother rose from her chair. "I'll take Annie for you."

Trembling, Pauline handed over the baby, who quieted the moment she saw Mother.

"There," Charles said, sitting down on the window seat to face them. "Now that we're all settled, I'd like to get to the point of my visit. I have a chance to buy the biggest tent in San Francisco, but I need financial help. The lender would double his money in no time at all."

"You want me to lend you money for a *gambling* tent?" Father asked, appalled.

"Just for a month or two."

"Never," Father said. His fists clenched, he moved closer to Charles. "Even if we had any money," he said evenly, "we wouldn't give it to you. Not after the way you treated Pauline."

For a moment Daniel was sure his father was going to throw Charles out. But Charles rose hurriedly and backed to the door. "I should have known not to count on help from *this* family!"

Pauline's blue eyes were brimming with tears. "Charles . . . please . . . you know how Uncle Franklin feels about gambling." She put out her hand as if pleading for him to understand.

"Don't preach to me!" Charles snapped. "And never mind helping me either. I'll get that tent one way or another." He darted a furious look at her and opened the courtyard door.

"For once, Charles Herrington, try to think about your family instead of yourself," Father said.

"I *am* thinking about them," Charles shot back. "That's why I'm trying to earn a living!" And, with that, he bade them a dramatic "Good day!" and slammed the door behind him.

As he watched Charles stride angrily through the courtyard, Daniel wished their wagon train had gone to Oregon as they had planned instead of coming to California. In fact, he wished they'd never heard of the gold rush. Almost as soon as the news of gold reached them on the trail, Charles declared he was heading for California. Father, feeling that God wanted him to keep the family together, had followed Charles, and here they were.

But if God wanted them to come here, Daniel thought, surely He must have plans for them—for *all* of them, including Charles Herrington.

CHAPTER 2

By morning, the rain had stopped, and Mother cooked outside on the veranda in a beehive shaped adobe oven called a *horno*. When they all sat down for breakfast at the plank kitchen table, they could smell trouble, beginning with the bacon and bread.

Father usually called Mother "Ruthie Sunshine," but today her sweet round face looked more like yesterday's storm clouds. She stood with her hands on her hips and complained, "I've cooked over firewood. I've cooked over sagebrush. I've even cooked over buffalo chips. But I've never cooked in a horno before, and I pray I won't ever be expected to do so again!"

"Why, Ruthie, this isn't like you at all!" Father exclaimed.

"It might be fine for the natives around here, but I miss my fine cookstove back home," she complained.

Father was not the only one who was surprised. Rarely had Daniel seen Mother upset enough to cry. She had re-mained calm and sunny throughout their long journey—

over miles of hot, barren desert, through blizzards and storms. She certainly never cried over "spilt milk," as she called it. But now, tears of frustration seemed ready to fall.

"I'll try to find a cookstove in town," Father promised. "It might take awhile, but we'll live a civilized life again. "

Tears glistened in Mother's blue eyes. "I'm sorry, dear. I'm ashamed to have lost my temper and ruined your breakfast on top of it."

Father patted her hand. "Things will be better soon. We loaded an empty trunk on the wagon to fill with provisions while we're in town. Just give us your list."

Daniel scraped the burned part off his biscuit and cut the black char from his bacon. The porridge tasted singed through and through, but he managed to eat some of it. As soon as possible, though, he excused himself.

"Where's Suzannah?" he asked Pauline as she brought Jamie to the kitchen for his breakfast.

"She looked so tired, I let her sleep."

"Suzannah . . . asleep at this hour?" He could hardly believe it.

His cousin still wasn't up by the time he and Father set off for town in the covered wagon. As they walked alongside the oxen, Father spoke solemnly. "San Francisco is a wild tent town, full of all kinds of people—most of them, I fear, folks who aim to get rich one way or the other. I'm sure there are some good people out here, but we'll be most likely to see the other kind in town—the drinkers and gamblers and troublemakers."

A curious mixture of fear and excitement tingled down Daniel's spine. Suppose they ran into real gunslingers, men wanted by the law? "Guess that's why you bought us a house in the countryside," he said.

"Exactly. San Francisco is no place for womenfolk and children right now."

Daniel could swear he heard a muffled laugh coming from the wagon, but there was nothing in it but the trunk and an old quilt. It was probably just the trunk slipping and sliding against the side.

Father went on as if he hadn't heard anything unusual. "Last year, San Francisco had two hundred buildings and five hundred people, and they say the population has more than doubled since then."

Daniel was only half-listening, still convinced there was something going on inside the wagon.

When they arrived in the foggy tent town, he was surprised to see how busy it was so early in the morning. Burly men hammered and sawed, throwing up crude buildings, and drunken singing blared from the gambling tents. The voices sang out, the words slurred:

Buffalo gals, won't you come out tonight,
  Come out tonight, come out tonight?
Buffalo gals, won't you come out tonight
  And dance by the light of the moon?

"Afraid some men are drinking already," Father remarked.

Daniel looked about for Charles, but he was nowhere to be seen. Instead, uncombed, unwashed loafers leaned against the buildings, some of them red-eyed from drink. Back home in Georgetown, Daniel had heard preachers speak against the evils of drinking and gambling, but he doubted there was much preaching going on in this place.

Litter and horse droppings lay all over the rutted street. As they passed, a bearded miner stomped from a tent store wearing a new red flannel shirt, and flung his old, tattered one into the road with the other litter.

Before long, Daniel and Father were picking their way between makeshift saloons and gambling tents where grizzled men wandered in and out. Inside, the men sang:

Oh what was your name in the States?
Was it Thompson or Johnson or Bates?
Did you murder your wife
And flee for your life?
Oh, what was your name in the States?

"Someone's even made up a song about the no-accounts who've escaped here," remarked Father. "San Francisco might be named for a saint, but it's not a saintly town, I fear. The fact is, there's more and more lawlessness and very few people who'll stand up against it."

Near the waterfront, seagulls cried and swooped over the hundreds of abandoned ships lying at anchor in the harbor, their masts tangled in a maze of ropes and rotting timbers. Strolling closer to the water's edge, Daniel could see the old Customs House, the only building left from Spanish days, standing like a sentry over the bay. Above, on a hillside, weathered frame buildings advertised "Beds," while farther up the steep slope, shanties had been hastily built of everything from rough boards to packing crates and flattened tin cans. All in all it was a sorry sight.

As the sun began to burn through the fog, San Francisco Bay emerged a brilliant blue. With the bright sun shining on the water, Daniel's spirits rose.

"Our lot's over there," Father pointed out, "not too far from the water. The problem is finding lumber for a building. I don't intend to build our store out of crates or tin cans."

"Am I glad to hear that!" Daniel shouted. "Hooray!"

"Hooray!" came an echo from the wagon.

Astonished, Daniel looked around to see a young boy crawl out of the arched opening and jump lightly to the ground. He was wearing Daniel's outgrown brown pants, rolled up at the cuff, his favorite calico shirt, and a wool cap pulled down over his ears.

Daniel couldn't believe his eyes. "Suzannah!"

She laughed. "A tin can store wouldn't suit you at all, Uncle Franklin. Not after your fine brick store in Georgetown."

Uncle Franklin stared too. "Suzannah Colton! What are you doing here? Pauline and your Aunt Ruthie will be worried sick."

"I left a note on my bed . . ." she replied, trying to act contrite, ". . . after plumping up the pillows to look like I was sound asleep."

"Guess we shouldn't be surprised," Daniel said. "Bet you thought you'd miss something exciting."

"That's the truth of it," she admitted. "And since Uncle Franklin said San Francisco was no place for *womenfolk,* I thought I'd better come as a *boy-folk!*"

Daniel laughed, even though Suzannah in boy's clothing was a disgrace.

Father couldn't quite hide his grin either. "Then see to it you stay in disguise, young lady, and lower your voice before curiosity gets the best of you yet."

Humph, Daniel thought, knowing Father was secretly pleased that Suzannah had such spunk. Sometimes on the wagon trail, she'd even led the oxen through the mountains. He did have one question for her though. "Where did you get my clothes?"

"Easy," she replied with a grin. "From the dirty clothes pile."

Father shook his head. "Well, as long as you're here, there's not much we can do about it, is there?"

"Just what she was counting on," Daniel remarked.

"Well, I *could* help with the shopping," Suzannah insisted. "Aunt Ruthie said she'd like red calico for the kitchen windows so everything in the house wouldn't be so 'all-fired white.' That would make her happy even if you can't find a stove."

"So you were eavesdropping this morning." Daniel said.

She elbowed him in the ribs and changed the subject, turning to gaze out over the shimmering blue water of the bay. "Why are those ships all atilt and bumping into each other out there? Boats were never allowed to anchor like that in Alexandria or Georgetown."

"They've been abandoned," Father explained.

"Remember the miners out at the gold diggings?" Daniel asked. "Lots were sailors who'd jumped ship and struck out to make their fortune. The holds of their ships are still crammed full of cargo. Father hopes to buy those goods and sell them in the store."

As they stood talking, a short, stout man wearing the uniform of a ship's captain approached. He walked with a wide step and a rolling gait, and his face was so brown that the small white beard on his chin resembled a tuft of cotton. "Ahoy, mates! You Franklin Colton?" he addressed Father.

"Indeed, I am."

The man pumped Father's hand. "Eliah Scully here, captain of the *Bostonia,* a Boston brig out in that infernal jam of ships. Heard you were planning to set up a store hereabouts."

"That's the plan. We're just down from the gold fields and eager to get started."

Captain Scully rubbed his white beard. "Been watching for you, wondering if your lot's for sale."

"No, I'm sorry to disappoint you," Father said. "I'm going to build a store on it."

Captain Scully let out a sigh. "Afraid you might say that. The thing is my ship's hold is full of cargo, and I'd like to sell it. Heard you had a store back in Georgetown, so I figured you'd know about such things."

Father nodded. "I've been a merchant all of my life, and my father before me."

"Then I have a proposal for you." The captain gave a nervous laugh. "You'll no doubt think it's peculiar, but . . . well, I thought we could ground my brig on your lot and open the doors for business. Call it the Boston Brig Store. It'd be different enough to attract a good bit of attention."

"Put your ship on my lot?" Father said, his green eyes wide.

The captain nodded, his beard bobbing. "It's an uncommon practice, I know, but uncommon ideas are often the best."

"But why on *my* lot?" Father asked, which was the question Daniel wanted to ask.

"It's just above the high tide line," the captain explained, "just right for groundin' a ship."

Father frowned in thought. "We-ll, it's not what I had in mind, but . . . now that I think of it, it might not be a bad idea at that. It would take some time to build a store and a good bit more gold that we have too. We could use your brig for the building, with your cargo as the merchandise, and be set up for business almost immediately." His voice rose as the idea grew on him. "What are you carrying aboard?"

Captain Scully pulled some papers from the inside pocket of his jacket and handed them over. "Here's the ship's manifest. It lists all the cargo, but I can tell you we're carryin' everything from pickles to pickaxes, from shovels to cookstoves."

"Cookstoves?" Father repeated, his eyes wide. "Did you say *cookstoves*?"

Daniel was equally amazed to hear the matter of cookstoves come up again so soon this morning.

"Yes, indeed," the captain replied. "First rate woodburnin' kitchen stoves. Best you can buy in all o' Boston."

"Let's go take a look," Father said. "But first, this is my son, Daniel. And this stowaway we just found in our wagon is my niece, Suzannah Colton, dressed in Daniel's old clothes."

Captain Scully's blue eyes danced with amusement. "The only way a girl should dress hereabouts. I like her already. Now, follow me and allow me to give you a tour of the *Bostonia*. What a store she could be in the hands of enterprisin' people! In fact, what a place California could be!"

As they spoke on, Daniel remembered Father's prayer before they'd left home—that God would give him clear guidance about what they should do. *Stoves!* And after Mother being so set on having one!

Captain Scully led them to a dinghy by the shore. They clambered aboard, and he rowed them out to his old wooden brig anchored in the midst of the other abandoned vessels.

"She's been idle for five months now," he said sadly, "ever since the sailors heard about gold in the hills. She'll make a fine store, she will. Best of all, I can stay in my cabin at night to guard the premises and have four other cabins to use as offices or for rent. With so few hotel rooms in town, I'll wager we'd have some takers."

"Another interesting idea," said Father, regarding the captain with admiration. "Seems you're more of a businessman than you thought. What concerns me most right now, though, is how to get a good-sized brig out of this tangle of abandoned ships . . . and then up to my lot."

Captain Scully threw back his head and laughed heartily. "And what would a landlubber like you know about that? You leave the sailin' to me, friend. We'll steer the brig into a deep channel and wait for high tide. Then we'll float her in as far as we can. After that, we'll tie ropes to trees and use the ship's capstan to wind the ship farther ashore."

"You make it sound easy," Daniel said.

" 'Course it's easy when you know what you're doin'," Captain Scully agreed. "I'll take charge of beachin' the *Bostonia* if your father will take charge of sellin' the ship's goods. It's really not as flighty as it sounds, since our 'tween deck was used for a store when we sailed the California coast. Customers walked right in off the docks. And when we lay at anchor, we rowed them out in the ship's longboats."

"It does sound ideal for walk-in trade," Father admitted.

Aboard the main deck of the old brig, Father shook his head. "It still boggles my mind to consider putting a ship ashore for a store."

"It's been done plenty of times before." Captain Scully gave a commanding wave. "Let me show you around."

After they had toured the main deck, they followed the captain down a set of narrow steps to a lower deck.

"I think I know how the 'tween deck got its name," Daniel observed, "from being *between* the main deck and the cargo hold on the ship's bottom."

"Right you are, lad!" The captain gave him a pleased smile.

As Daniel stepped onto the 'tween deck, he looked around. There was enough light streaming down through the hatch that he could make out the ship's store—shelves and counters with bags of beans and rice wedged between them.

After they'd looked over the ship's store, Father said, "Now I'd like to see those stoves you were talking about down in the cargo hold."

———◆◆———

The wagon bearing Daniel, Suzannah, and Father rolled into Rancho Encino as darkness was falling.

"Stay here while I fetch your mother and Pauline to see what we've brought," Father said, grinning his famous Colton grin. "Be ready to whip open the back flaps the minute I tell you."

Shortly, Daniel and Suzannah could see the flicker of lantern light as Father escorted the two women from the house.

"You mean Suzannah dressed in Daniel's clothes and stowed away in the wagon?" Mother asked. "She told us in her note she'd be with you, but we—"

"That's not all," Father replied. "Our new store will soon be ready to open for business, *and* there's something in the wagon for you—a gift from my new partner, Captain Eliah Scully!

"Store? Partner?" She blinked, unable to take in all the news at once.

"Now!" Father yelled, and Daniel and Suzannah moved around to the back and flung open the canvas flaps. In the lantern light, the black iron cookstove towered on its pedestal like a throne, its silver trim gleaming.

Mother's mouth dropped open. "A stove! A beautiful, wonderful, civilized stove!"

Daniel stared as his mother threw her arms around Father. The next thing he knew, Father had picked Mother up and was whirling her around.

"Oh, Franklin!" she protested. "The children! Besides, you'll hurt your back. Now put me down."

Father only laughed and gave her another whirl for good measure.

The moment Mother was on her feet, Suzannah spoke up. "I talked them into buying some cloth for kitchen curtains,

Aunt Ruthie. The kitchen won't look so all-fired white with red calico at the windows."

Mother gave Suzannah a stern look. "I must have a word with you, young lady. I can't believe you'd go about in boys' clothing. But we'll take that up later. Right now, I want to examine this stove and then that red calico."

Daniel helped her climb into the wagon and she touched the shiny black stove almost as if it might vanish before her eyes. "Oh, Franklin, it has a warming oven and a water reservoir. And to think . . ." she went on, her voice soft, "I prayed for one this very morning."

Father gazed at her tenderly. "And I prayed for clear guidance and got it through a cookstove."

God surely answers prayer in surprising ways, Daniel thought. When he grinned at Suzannah, he could tell she must have been thinking the same thing, for she burst into laughter. *A stove and a store on a Boston brig all in the same day!*

CHAPTER 3

As they stood laughing and talking, Daniel heard the sound of horses and the rattle of wagon wheels coming toward them on the road.

"Ho, Franklin Colton!" someone called out. "This the Colton place?"

"That it is!" Father called back.

Daniel recognized the man's voice at once. "It's Uncle Karl and his family! And here come Lad and Lass!"

Aunt Pearl's collie dogs barked a greeting and jumped up on Daniel, overjoyed to see him again. They licked his face as he knelt down to pet them. "You're home," he told them. "There's a fine barn for you, with not a cat around!"

Moments later, the others pulled up in front of the house—Uncle Karl on horseback, Cousin Garth driving the oxen, and Aunt Pearl riding in their covered wagon. Bringing up the rear were fifteen-year-old Ned Taylor and

Octavius Brooks, better known as Big Red, a fine man who had befriended them in the gold fields.

Even in the lantern light, anyone could see that Aunt Pearl was as blond as Mother, only younger and thinner.

"We had trouble with a wagon wheel," she said, "and then we didn't think we'd find your place at night—" She stared across into the back of their wagon. "Why, it's a stove, Ruthie!"

Mother laughed. "It's a miracle, Pearl, that's what it is! I've burned everything I've tried to cook in the outdoor oven this livelong day, and Franklin just brought me this new cookstove from town."

"Looks like you found a good house too . . . another miracle with so many folks movin' west," said Big Red, his hair and beard as red as Daniel remembered. "Can we give you a hand carryin' the stove to the kitchen?"

Daniel grinned. It was just like Big Red to pitch in. Out in the gold fields, he'd helped them start a restaurant and had even bought the log cabins across the road with his own money so they'd have a roof over their heads until Pauline's baby was born.

"We'd be most grateful for your help, friend," Father said. "And there's room in our house to sleep everyone."

"I'd be glad to sleep in the barn," Ned Taylor offered, his mop of bright red curls shining. Back in Missouri, he'd been hired to drive the loose livestock for the wagon train.

"There's an extra cot in my room," Daniel said. "How about bunking with me?" He sure hoped Ned would agree, or he'd likely end up rooming with Cousin Garth, a thought Daniel didn't relish.

"How about me?" Garth asked, his dark brows furrowed. "Where am I sleepin'?"

"We thought you could share a room with Big Red," Father told him. "We'll get it all worked out once we get this stove in the kitchen and the livestock in the barn."

"I'm ready to help," Aunt Pearl said. She caught up her blue gingham skirt and jumped down from the wagon.

Once again Daniel wondered how someone so pretty and young-looking could have settled for a gruff codger like Uncle Karl. Mother claimed that after Aunt Pearl's first husband and two children died from the fever, she'd been so grieved that she'd married the first man to come along.

As soon as they arrived in the courtyard, Pauline hurried out to greet the newcomers and marvel over the cookstove. Before long, she was holding the kitchen door open as the men muscled the huge black stove inside. When the stove was finally in place, they all stood back to admire it.

"I've got a stew simmering in that awful horno oven," Mother said. "Let's hope it's not burned to a crisp. Pearl, will you rescue it, then help me put away the other provisions the men brought back from town?"

"I'd better check on Annie," Pauline said. "And Suzannah, you get out of that awful garb and into a dress! What in the world would Mama and Papa say if they could see you now?"

Daniel stayed in the kitchen to help Big Red attach the flue between the stove and the window. "I hope you don't mind bunking with Garth," he said. "I know he's *my* relative, but I don't think he likes me very much."

"Don't bother me none," Big Red replied with a kindly smile. "Garth's comin' along, thanks to Aunt Pearl's kindness. He's not near as mean as when I first met him. Expect the Lord has somethin' special in mind for him."

Daniel let out a long sigh, discouraged with himself. Ever since he'd witnessed to Ned Taylor on the trail and watched Ned accept Jesus as his Savior, Daniel had felt God might be calling him to a special work for Him, like being a preacher or a missionary. Yet here he was, avoiding his own stepcousin. And everyone who knew Garth Stengler knew *he* needed the Lord!

"Besides," Big Red went on, "you and Ned are such good friends."

Daniel nodded as he held the metal stove flue in place. Ned was the best friend he'd ever had, maybe partly because he'd also saved the older boy from drowning during the Kansas River crossing on the trek west.

Daniel and Big Red had finished fastening the flue to the stove when Pauline returned to the kitchen with baby Annie, bundled up in her yellow blankets. "Jamie's still sleeping," she said. "He was all worn out from exploring the house."

Big Red's brown eyes glowed when he saw her with the baby. "What a picture the two of you make . . . like the Madonna and child." He wiped his hands on the seat of his pants, then asked a little timidly, "Reckon I could hold little Annie for a spell?"

Pauline smiled. "Of course you may, Octavius."

He blushed and ducked his head. No one but Pauline ever called him by his given name.

The big man took Annie and cradled her easily. He took a seat on the bench built along the wall, and Pauline settled down beside him, watching as he marveled at the baby's rosebud mouth and tiny fingers.

Why couldn't Charles love his own baby like that? Daniel wondered. And why couldn't he be as kind as Big Red?

Daniel kept his thoughts to himself. "Guess I'll wash up for supper."

Big Red stood up right away, handing Annie back to Pauline. "Guess I'd better be shovin' off too."

An hour later, all twelve of them took their places around the big oak dining table. Suzannah had already set the table, and Mother and Aunt Pearl brought in a huge pot of stew and ladled it into soup bowls.

"Well, I must be slipping," Father teased. "You're not serving me a burnt offering this evening!"

"Franklin Colton!" Mother scolded, her blue eyes flashing. "In all the years we've been married, you know I've seldom burned the dinner!"

"True," he admitted. "You're a fine cook and a fine wife. And the stew smells delicious!"

They smiled at each other, and before things got too mushy, Daniel spoke up. "Bet this stew would have been burned if it had spent another minute in that horno oven."

"Then we'll thank God for His timing!" laughed Father. "That new stove arrived just in the nick of time. Now let's bow our heads for grace."

Daniel scooted over so he wouldn't crowd Suzannah on the plank bench, his eyes still open as Father began to pray. In that fleeting moment, he noticed that all heads were bowed except for Cousin Garth's and Uncle Karl's. Cousin Garth seemed a little uncomfortable, but Uncle Karl looked downright angry.

After supper, everyone else moved into the parlor to talk. Suzannah was alone in the kitchen putting away the clean dishes when Daniel came in. "I'd give anything to watch them beach Captain Scully's brig," she told him. "Boys have all the fun."

"Well, why don't you talk Aunt Pearl into coming to town that day?"

Suzannah's blue-green eyes lit up. "Daniel Colton, sometimes I like your ideas!"

On the day they were to begin work on the waterfront property, Daniel rode Chessie, a chestnut gelding they had acquired with the ranch property. "Come on," he urged, "we're going to raise a store from the water."

Riding beside him, Ned Taylor laughed.

"You laughin' at me?" asked Uncle Karl as he rode by on Gray.

Daniel nudged Chessie with his knees. "No, sir. We're just laughing at the idea of having a ship for a store."

"Strikes me as a harebrained idea," his uncle grumbled. "Never done nothin' like that in Missouri."

"That's not the only laughin' we'll hear," Garth added. "We'll be laughed clear outta town!"

"Maybe and maybe not," Big Red said. "New places and new times call for new ideas."

Uncle Karl was not convinced. "I'll do my part gettin' the store ready, but I'd rather work on a farm."

"I've been meaning to ask you about that, Karl," Father said. "After the store's running in town, what would you and Garth think about taking over the farm?"

Uncle Karl glowered under his bushy brows. "Mebbe. Only 'til spring though. Don't forgit that, come dry weather, we're headin' back to the gold fields."

"Until spring then," Father said agreeably. "Big Red grew up on a farm in Pennsylvania, and he'd like to work both until he finds out what suits him best."

"That right?" Daniel called back to Big Red, who was bringing up the rear on his brown horse.

Big Red grinned. "Never thought I'd want to go back to farmin' again, but I like these *ranchos* out here."

Before long, they were riding through the muddy streets of San Francisco. It seemed to Daniel that even more tents and shacks had gone up since yesterday, which wasn't surprising since three new ships jammed with goldseekers had sailed in overnight.

The fog over the bay was lifting, revealing sparkling waters that reflected the fleecy clouds overhead. Daniel couldn't help thinking again that San Francisco itself might look pretty shabby, but the view was splendid. Yes, this town had possibilities.

When they arrived at Father's waterfront lot, Captain Scully's hired laborers were already hard at work digging out a spot for the ship on the upward slope. The captain had roped off the section of land to be leveled for the brig, and a space up the middle for a deep channel to hold the ship's keel.

"Ahoy, mates!" he called out. "Grab a shovel and dig! We have to float in the *Bostonia* at high tide in three days." Despite being short and stout, the captain had a way of taking command with the wave of a hand.

Daniel picked up a shovel and turned over some sandy soil. "Captain Scully doesn't waste time."

"Well, he'd better do some more thinkin', if you ask me," Uncle Karl muttered. "We're gonna have to lay down some plankin' to the gangway or folks'll mire up to their necks in this mud."

"There's wood down in the hold," the captain said, overhearing him. "All we need to do is break up a few crates and barrels." He squinted at Uncle Karl. "I'd wager you're just the man to supervise the operation."

Uncle Karl nodded. "We'll have to run drains so winter storms don't wash this brig right back into San Francisco Bay."

Daniel set to work with the others. They shoveled sand and dirt all morning, scarcely stopping to eat the ham and biscuits Mother and Aunt Pearl had sent along. Every once in a while, Daniel glanced around for Charles. There was no sign of him among the bystanders who came to watch and ask questions.

At noon Father sent Daniel out to buy supplies and food for the workers. "If we treat them right," Father said, "they'll know we hope to be a force for good in this town."

Daniel drove a wagon to the nearest stores set up in ramshackle warehouses along the waterfront.

While he waited for his order to be packaged, Charles ambled into the store. Daniel nodded at him uneasily.

"What's going on out at your property?" Charles asked. "Digging for buried treasure?"

"You might say that," Daniel replied. "We're planning to ground the *Bostonia* and turn her into a store."

Charles snorted in disgust. "That's the most ridiculous scheme I've heard yet."

Daniel shrugged. "Nobody asked you," he said under his breath, then changed the subject. "What are you in town for?"

For an instant it appeared that Charles wouldn't answer. Then he snapped, "Raising funds for my gambling tent, since none of my so-called family would help me!" He turned on his heel and strode toward the back of the store.

Daniel was glad to finish his own business and get out before Charles decided to ask more questions.

———————◆◆◆———————

Three days later, the digging at Father's waterfront lot was almost complete, and the *Bostonia* stood at anchor near the shore.

Just after two o'clock, Captain Scully said, "The tide comes in in 'bout an hour—as high a tide as we'll have for a while."

Daniel's hands were blistered, but he shoveled all the harder with the others until finally the channel was deep enough to hold the keel of the old brig.

"As soon as the *Bostonia* floats in on the tide, we'll throw out ropes," Captain Scully said. "Tie 'em to the trees. Then we'll haul her in to her new berth."

Daniel looked around as the captain and a few of his workmen climbed into the dinghy to row out to the ship. It seemed that everyone in town had gathered to see the *Bostonia's* last voyage. Men had come on foot and on horseback, and there was even one covered wagon rolling to a stop at the edge of the crowd.

Looking closer, Daniel saw a young boy driving the oxen. The lad was wearing Daniel's clothes and his brown cap was pulled down over his ears. *Suzannah!* Even more astonishing, riding in the wagon were two "fellows" whose faces resembled Aunt Pearl's and Mother's! He stared, dumbfounded, until Suzannah flapped an arm and shook her head with a warning scowl.

"Ahoy!" Captain Scully bellowed from the ship's bow and raised a fist skyward. "Make way ashore, you landlubbers! Make way for the brig *Bostonia!*"

As the tide rolled in, the old brig rode proudly in the water toward them.

"Here come the ropes!" the captain shouted as his men flung them ashore.

Father and Big Red caught them, then ran to tie them around two towering trees.

"Now, haul away, mates!" Captain Scully yelled. He and his men manned the ship's capstan, and the *Bostonia* slid along in the sand toward its new home. As soon as the old brig settled into place, Daniel and the others shoveled dirt around its keel and packed it down.

"Hurrah!" the crowd shouted, some tossing their hats into the air. "Three cheers for the *Bostonia!* Hip-hip-hooray! Hip-hip-hooray! Hip-hip-hooray!"

In the midst of the cheering, Suzannah stepped forward. She handed a big wooden sign to Father and gestured toward the wagon. He was so astounded to see Mother and Aunt Pearl sitting there, dressed in his and Uncle Karl's clothes, that his mouth dropped open.

For a long moment, he could only stare at them until Suzannah spoke to him. He examined the sign they had brought with them, then hoisted it high above his head for all to see; *BOSTON BRIG EMPORIUM.*

"*Emporium* was Daniel's idea," Suzannah explained. "It had to be a name as eye-catching as a ship that's been turned into a store!"

"Good for him!" Father exclaimed. "*Emporium* says it all. That means we sell anything!"

"Three cheers for the Boston Brig Emporium!" Big Red shouted.

This time Daniel and his whole family—including Uncle Karl and Garth—joined in. "Hip-hip-hooray! Hip-hip-hooray! Hip-hip-hooray!"

The squat brig perched on land was a comical sight, Daniel decided, far different from their fine brick building in Georgetown. But, for better or for worse, they now had a store in the California Territory.

He looked out at the cheering crowd. To his amazement, Charles stood at the edge. But he wasn't cheering. Instead, he eyed the transplanted ship thoughtfully. Then, noticing that Daniel had seen him, he hurried away.

CHAPTER 4

Captain Scully's men let down the wooden gangway from the *Bostonia's* deck, and Daniel helped to settle it firmly on the muddy ground. Walking up the planking, he checked the ship for damage. "It's a wonder she didn't break up."

The captain threw back his head and laughed, his small white beard blowing in the breeze. "Groundin' her was nothing compared to sailin' around Cape Horn in a storm, lad. This old brig was built to last."

Prospective customers already crowded the gangway. "What cargo ye carryin'?" they called out. "Got any decent food aboard?" "Any shoes or boots fer sale?"

"Aye, all that and more!" called the captain. "We've got just about anything you might be lookin' for—tea and coffee, spices and molasses, hardware, crockery, shoes and boots, cloth for sewin', furniture, tents, cookstoves, ready-made suits, and dresses for the ladies!"

At that moment Father stepped up and hung a heavy chain at the top of the gangway to keep the customers from boarding the ship before they were ready. "Please, folks, just give us some time to get the stock ready, and we'll be open for business."

Using the *Bostonia* as a store still struck Daniel as odd. The ships that sailed into Georgetown had sold their goods to warehouses and stores—not to walk-in customers. If only Suzannah could have stayed to help, but she and Mother and Aunt Pearl had gone home with the wagon, probably still laughing at the surprise on Father's and Uncle Karl's faces when they were recognized.

On the main deck, the captain's helpers wrestled off the cargo hatch cover, and Daniel hurried with the others down the steps to the 'tween deck. "I didn't think of it yesterday," he said, "but with the shelves and counters, this looks like a country store."

Captain Scully nodded. "Exactly how some folks saw it when we sailed up the California coast. But bein' in one place will make things a lot easier. Still, it saddens me to think that the old brig will never sail the high seas again."

Daniel's eyes shone. "I expect it was a great adventure."

"Aye, lad. Many a tale could be told 'bout the *Bostonia* in her early days—pirates, sunken treasure, even mutiny." He squinted his eyes, gazing far out across the sparkling waters of the bay to the place where the sky met the sea.

Daniel's heart raced. Maybe someday the captain would tell some of his stories. Daniel had always loved the sea. Why, if God wasn't calling him to be a preacher or maybe a missionary, he'd love to be a sailor!

There was no time for regrets for either of them though, not with so many customers waiting outside. Some of them were so caught up in the excitement that they were already helping Uncle Karl and Garth lay down a cratewood walk between the road and the gangway.

Inside the brig, Daniel and Ned lit lanterns to add to the light streaming down the hatch and set to work. As Captain Scully's hired workers lugged huge wooden crates from the cargo hold, Big Red pried them open with a crowbar, and Daniel and Ned stocked the shelves.

Before long, tins of oysters, sardines, crackers, hard candies, and other foodstuffs lined the shelves. Next, they rolled out barrels of pickles, sugar, and flour. The huge bags of rice and beans needed only to be untied.

As soon as the 'tween deck was set up, Father turned to the captain. "Shall we put shoes and boots up on the main deck? With such a crowd out there, it would give the customers more space to try them on."

"You're the man who knows about shopkeepin'," Captain Scully replied. "My supercargo jumped ship with the sailors. He's probably up to his knees in mud out at the gold fields right now, when he could be living high and dry here in charge of a boomin' ship's store."

Father laughed. "Well, I must say *I* never expected to be a supercargo, but since it appears that's what I am, I'd recommend roping off a section of the main deck for footwear, tools, tents, and hardware."

Uncle Karl had just come up for more wood when Father asked, "Could you take charge of selling on the main deck this afternoon?"

Puzzled, Uncle Karl paused. "You mean, you want *me?* You know I don't know nothin' 'bout storekeepin'."

Father gave him a fine smile. "It just takes common sense, and you've plenty of that, Karl Stengler."

When Uncle Karl's mouth turned up in a hint of a smile too, he looked so different that Daniel could almost see why Aunt Pearl had married him. For a moment, the glittering black eyes softened, the deep lines carved into his face relaxed, and the heavy dark brows, usually pulled together in a frown, arched upward.

But it didn't take long for his face to droop once more. "Then I'll need Garth with me to keep an eye out for ruffians. Expect there's plenty of miners down on their luck who'd try anythin' to get out of payin' for their goods."

"Fine," Father said. "I'll set up as cashier by the gangway so they'll have to pay on their way out. Daniel, Ned, and Big Red will wait on customers in the ship's store on the 'tween deck. Captain, you can help by keeping the customers orderly while they're waiting in line and checking their receipts when they leave. We'll give them fair prices, but they'll have to treat us fairly too, if this business is to succeed."

"Aye-aye!" Captain Scully gave Father a smart salute. "I'll maintain order and check the receipts."

After an hour of hard work, Father surveyed the shelves. "We've enough goods on the shelves to get started, and Captain Scully has found the cashier's box and bags for gold dust, so let's open the store."

The captain mounted the steps to the main deck, then rang the ship's brass bell. "Ahoy! All hands aboard!" he called out. "The Boston Brig Emporium is open for business! Shoes, boots, tents, and such on the main deck. Foodstuffs, shirts, and smaller goods on the 'tween deck."

"Hooray!" the miners shouted. "Hip-hip-hooray!"

Daniel watched the first customers swarm down the steps into the ship's store. He had helped Father in the store in

Georgetown, but never in a crush like this. The men jostled each other rudely and reached over the counters, trying to pluck the goods from the shelves.

"I'll be glad to take your order," Daniel repeated over and over, but the eager customers ignored him.

In his most commanding voice, Father spoke up, "Gentlemen, if you'll line up in an orderly manner in front of our clerks, they'll be glad to assist you with your needs."

Slowly the men quieted down and formed lines in front of Daniel, Ned, and Big Red. Daniel's first customer was a bleary-eyed fellow in a tattered red miner's shirt and a mud-spattered hat, recently back from the gold fields, no doubt, for he said, "I'd give ye a good-sized nugget for a dill pickle. I've got a fearful hankerin' for pickles."

Daniel choked back a laugh. "A good-sized gold nugget will buy *plenty* of pickles! You'll find fair prices marked right on the pickle barrel."

"Fair prices?" the customer repeated. "First I heerd o' fair prices since I come to this Californy Territory."

"Well, you'll find them here," Daniel said. "We hope you'll be coming back to buy again."

The man eyed him with suspicion. "Next thing ye'll be tellin' me ye're closed on the Sabbath."

Daniel nodded, for just last night, Father had suggested that very thing. "Yes, sir. We will be closed on the Sabbath. But you're welcome to attend our worship services at *Rancho Encino,* outside of town. And welcome to stay for dinner too."

"Well, I'll be!" the man declared, scratching his shaggy beard. "Never heerd the likes of it in these parts!"

"Got any flannel shirts?" asked a miner. "Ready-made, like they make 'em in New York?"

"Right here," Daniel said. "Ready-made flannel shirts, but these are from Boston. What size do you need?"

When they found the right size, the miner pulled off his own filthy rag of a shirt and put on the new one, then tossed the old one over the counter. "It's yours fer swabbin' the deck."

"Ye got any candy fer Christmas?"

The unexpected request caught Daniel short. *Christmas!* he thought in surprise as he put three different tins of hard candy on the counter to give the miner a choice. They'd been so busy getting settled in their new house and establishing their store that they'd forgotten Christmas was just around the corner.

"I'll take all three tins," the miner decided, pulling out his bag of gold dust.

The moment he left, Daniel hid two tins of candy under the counter to buy for his own family for Christmas. At least he'd have something set aside to give them.

Business remained brisk. The customers had plenty of gold dust to spend on goods at fair prices, and they liked the idea of shopping on an old brig.

By six o'clock, the sun was sinking into the bay and the shelves were almost empty. When Daniel ran up to the main deck to ask his father a question, he saw that many of the tents, pickaxes, and boots had been sold too. Nearby Garth was still searching for the correct size boots for a customer.

"Your family is worth its salt, lad," said Captain Scully, beaming broadly.

"Thank you, sir," Daniel replied. "The Lord expects us to give a good day's work, so that's what we try to do." Noticing that Garth had overheard the conversation, he wondered what his stepcousin made of what he called "religious talk." But, for once, the older boy seemed willing to let it pass without making a sarcastic remark.

Captain Scully gave a nod of approval. "I believe we'll get on well as partners."

"Especially since you don't sell rum and other hard drink," Daniel said.

The captain lifted his white eyebrows. "Sold it all off last night, as a matter of fact. When I think of the mischief caused by Demon Rum in this town, I have to agree with your father."

A peculiar notion struck Daniel. "Who bought the hard drink?"

"A fellow from Virginia who's tryin' to open a gamblin' tent in town."

"Charles Herrington?"

"Aye, lad, that's the one. When he opens up, he's goin' to call his place 'The Herrington Palace.' You know him?"

Daniel nodded regretfully. "He's my cousin Pauline's husband. I'd . . . uh . . . I'd better get back to the store."

As he returned to the 'tween deck, he mulled over the news. Charles was still planning to open his gambling tent. Daniel wondered how and where he'd gotten the money to buy hard drink. Still, Charles must not have enough yet to open his tent. When he did, Daniel supposed, it wouldn't be long before the man would be in trouble again.

Down on the 'tween deck, he heard the ship's bell. "All hands ashore!" the captain shouted. "Closin' time is six bells! Bring your goods and receipts to the cashier on the main deck. We open again on Monday. All hands ashore!"

When the miners were gone, Father weighed the gold dust and nuggets they'd taken in. Even Captain Scully was amazed at the day's proceeds. "It's a far cry from bein' paid in tallow and smelly steer hides like we used to be on the California coast!" he told them.

"Humph! Some of them miners don't smell much better'n steer hides though," Uncle Karl remarked.

Everyone laughed, and Daniel saw Garth dart a proud glance at his father for making a joke. It was good to see the two of them feeling a part of things on this first day, even if they did choose to go back to the gold fields in the spring. In fact, the longer he was around them, the better Daniel liked his uncle and stepcousin.

Father also seemed pleased. "We'll take part of our profits to buy these boys some new white shirts, suits, and shoes," he said. "They've outgrown their clothes on the trip west, and tomorrow's our first Sabbath service."

Garth cast a half-worried, half-hopeful look toward his father, and Daniel wondered if Uncle Karl would go along with the idea.

"Reckon you'll earn it," Uncle Karl said in a gruff voice, then began to pick up the goods that had been flung about on the deck.

Big Red nodded. "Believe I'll buy myself some new duds too. I'm gettin' tired of lookin' like a scarecrow. We'd best dress halfway decent if we expect other folks to buy our stuff."

Besides, Daniel thought, Big Red would be preaching the sermon at their house tomorrow morning. He knew that to be true, because Big Red had asked him to read the Scriptures.

"Wonder if I could chance buying Suzannah a ready-made dress," Father said. "There's a blue one that looks about her size."

After they were outfitted, they tidied up the place and got ready to lock up for the night, carrying unsold goods down the hatch to store for the next business day. The captain left with the bags of gold dust, and when he returned, Daniel had a question for him.

"What's to keep other ships from stealing our idea and turning into stores like the *Bostonia*?"

"A few might try it," the old man replied. "But most of 'em aren't owned by their captains like I own the *Bostonia*. It'd take a nervy sailor to ground someone else's ship. Men have walked the plank for less."

Ned gave a laugh. "When I left Missouri to drive the livestock for the covered wagon train, I never dreamed I'd turn into a goldminer or a clerk on a grounded brig. Wonder what I'll be doin' next?"

Back up on the main deck, they had just folded their new clothes to take home when they heard someone drop the heavy chain at the top of the ship's gangway.

"Hands up!" barked a husky voice.

The command struck Daniel like a bolt of lightning, and his hands shot up. He turned slowly and saw two figures emerging from the darkness.

Moving into the lantern light, Daniel could see that the two men were pointing huge guns, their barrels aimed directly at the small group. Red bandanas hid the lower half of their faces, and western hats, jammed down low, allowed only a slit for their eyes. The two were wearing miners' clothing—flannel shirts, rough pants, and tall black boots.

"Hands up!" the man snarled again. He pointed his gun at Big Red, who'd been slower than the others to obey the order.

Big Red did as he was told. "What can we do for you gentleman?" he asked in a kind voice.

The man waved his gun at Daniel. "You, boy . . . the gold!"

"I-I don't have it!" he said in alarm, his upraised arms suddenly feeling limp and weak.

"Get it!"

Big Red took a step forward. "We've all worked mighty hard for that gold. The owners spent a lot hirin' workers to ground this ship here and—"

"Quiet!" the man warned in a menacing voice. "Boy, get gold . . . *now!*"

There was no mistaking the man's meaning, and Daniel felt a shiver of fear tingle down his spine. But he was angry too. These robbers meant to take everything they had worked long and hard for. Well, they wouldn't get away with it.

Captain Scully, who was standing beside Daniel, shook his head firmly. "This boy don't know where the gold is. And what's more, he couldn't even open the ship's safe if he found it. Come along, and I'll get it for you. But we'll need more light below," said the captain, heading for the hatch.

"Boy, carry light," ordered the other robber.

One of the robbers nodded permission, then gave Daniel a shove. Hands still in the air, Daniel backed away slowly and turned as carefully as he could. Stepping forward, he unhooked the nearest lantern, feeling its warmth beneath his wrist. Maybe he could somehow use the lantern as a weapon—but he quickly rejected that idea. All he'd do was set the place on fire! Best to go along with these pirates for now and look for a chance to get the better of them later.

Going down the steps, Captain Scully whispered, "No need for heroics, Daniel. We'll give them the gold and be done with it. Better to live and work another day."

It seemed like a bad dream . . . thieves stepping out of the darkness . . . one following him and Captain Scully down the stairs, waiting to take their money. He wondered if Captain Scully had a trick in mind. Maybe if they tripped him or something, Father, Big Red, and the others could handle the other one up on the main deck.

On the forward side of the 'tween deck, a passageway led to the captain's and officers' cabins. Daniel followed Captain Scully, trying to think fast. The captain had said, "No heroics," but it wasn't fair for these men to take the day's earnings. When he darted a glance behind him, the robber shoved the gun between his shoulder blades. Daniel shuddered and hurried along.

"Here's my cabin," Captain Scully told them. He stopped, got out his key, and unlocked the door.

The captain probably had a gun in the ship's safe, Daniel thought. As soon as the safe was open, he'd drop to the floor so Captain Scully could shoot. Suddenly it hit Daniel that, instead of trusting God to help them, he was actually hoping for a chance to *kill* a man! *Lord, help us,* he prayed. *And forgive me for not turning to Thee first—*

Inside, the cabin was dark. But the mahogany walls and brass fittings came to life, gleaming in the glow of the lantern light. Captain Scully headed for the ship's safe, and Daniel held his breath, feeling the hard steel of the robber's gun still pressing into his back.

Captain Scully cast a glance at them as he bent down by the safe, then spun the combination lock back and forth until the door swung open. Though the contents were hidden from view, Daniel half-expected the captain to grab a gun and turn around, armed.

But the captain calmly reached inside and withdrew a bag. "Here's the gold," he said. "Want me to carry it up to the deck?"

The masked man grunted and reached for the sack.

Now! thought Daniel. Surely now Captain Scully would pull his gun from the safe!

Instead, the captain closed the door of the safe and twirled the dial.

"Key!" the robber growled.

Captain Scully drew a weary breath and handed him the key to the cabin. The man grabbed it, then pointed to the bed sheet on the captain's bunk. As usual, his speech was clipped and brief. "Tear up!"

The captain pulled the sheet loose and began to rip it into long strips. When he'd finished, the robber instructed both of them to tie their own ankles together tightly, then for Captain Scully to tie Daniel's wrists behind his back. Finally, the thief tied the captain's wrists, stuffed a gag in their mouths, and blew out the lantern.

A second later, the cabin door closed behind him, leaving them in pitch-black darkness, and they heard the key turn in the lock.

Daniel lost no time in working his wrists back and forth, quickly discovering that the captain had left some slack. Within minutes, he had twisted one hand free of the cloth, then the other. Pulling the gag from his mouth, he worked quietly in the darkness to release the captain.

"Whew!" Captain Scully whispered with relief when Daniel had removed his gag and untied his hands. "Pirates

. . . even on land! You'd think he'd guess I keep an extra key, but he didn't strike me as any too smart."

"Think my father and the others are safe?" Daniel asked, listening to the clomping of boots overhead.

"We can hope so, lad. . . . I doubt those two want to do much shootin' and bring out the whole town to see what's happenin'."

Removing the last of the bindings from their ankles, Captain Scully felt for the lantern and lit it. Daniel blinked as light filled the cabin.

"Never hurts to have an extra key," the captain said, "or an extra hiding place for gold."

"You mean they didn't get all of it?" Daniel asked.

The captain held a finger to his lips. "Only half, lad," he whispered, then quietly opened the cabin door.

The clomping about on the main deck had stopped.

Slowly Daniel and Captain Scully crept up the stairway. When they arrived on top, the robbers were getting away on their horses through the dark night. And Father, Garth, Big Red, and Uncle Karl were wrestling with their bindings.

Safe! Daniel thought. *If nothing else, we're safe! Thank you, Lord!*

CHAPTER 5

Sunday morning, the gloomy mood brought on by the robbery lifted during the worship service in the parlor. "We have to forgive those who rob us and treat us bad, and we have to pray for our enemies," Big Red told them. "God loves those fellows too."

It was a struggle, but in the end, Daniel was able to pray for the two robbers who had given them such a scare. Later, at dinner, they all decided to try to forget about the robbery, count their blessings instead, and truly begin to celebrate Christmas.

In the afternoon, Daniel set out in the covered wagon with Suzannah, Garth, and Ned to find a Christmas tree somewhere on the wooded hillsides. Thick gray clouds threatened rain, and they hurried the oxen along.

Barking, Lad and Lass bounded ahead with Ned and Suzannah, and Daniel walked alongside the oxen with Garth. The two found little to say to each other, but it was fine to walk along quietly and listen to the familiar sounds of the creaking harness and the rattle of wagon wheels while the wind whistled about them.

"Expect Pa and me are better off here than in them gold hills now," Garth said at last.

"Wouldn't be surprised," Daniel agreed. "It's probably knee-deep in snow."

"I feel uneasy though," Garth went on, "like I'm wastin' time, and other folks is findin' *my* gold."

"*Your* gold?"

Garth nodded. "You know, all of the gold I'd be findin' if I was there."

"I doubt there's much going on this time of year," Daniel said. "There won't be enough water in the streams for panning either, not until the spring melt."

But Garth would not be comforted. "Don't know what's wrong with me," he complained. "I like it here all right . . . but I have an itch to be someplace else too—"

"Sounds like you need an anchor."

"An anchor?"

Daniel paused, selecting his words carefully. "An anchor like the *Bostonia* needed out in the bay. Something to hold you steady while life's swirling around you."

Garth's brown eyes narrowed. "You're talkin' about God, ain't you?"

"He's *my* anchor, all right," Daniel admitted.

Garth glanced at him as they walked beside the wagon. "I been watchin' your family and my stepmother, Pearl, too. You've all got somethin' like my . . . ma . . . had. Somethin' to hang on to. It's hard to believe God cares much about us though, not after them Injuns killed her. She wasn't hurtin' nobody, just hangin' out wash on the clothesline. If God's so good, why did He let that happen?" he finished bitterly.

"Our pastor in Georgetown says God sees death differently from the way we do," Daniel explained. "We think it's the end of everything, but for believers, it's the beginning of a whole new life in glory with Christ." He watched his stepcousin think it over.

"I don't know," Garth said. "I've tried to forgive them Injuns, but I just can't do it. I can't stop hatin' 'em for what they done—"

"I wouldn't be able to forgive on my own either," Daniel replied gently, seeing his stepcousin's pain. "When I need to forgive, I ask God to give me His love in place of the mean feeling I have for the one who's hurt me."

"You mean . . . I'd have to ask for God's love to come between me and them Injuns?"

Daniel nodded. "His love and His forgiveness . . ." He paused, "But it won't work if you don't have Christ in your heart."

"Hey, you down there!" Suzannah called from the top of a nearby hill. "I've found the perfect Christmas tree! It's too tall for the parlor, but we can cut some off the bottom."

"Coming!" Daniel called back. He would have liked to continue the discussion with his stepcousin, but Garth was already rushing up the hillside.

The tree was a Monterey pine, and maybe not too tall for the parlor's high wooden ceiling. While Ned chopped it down, Suzannah asked, "Now that we have a tree, how are we going to decorate it? We don't have any little candles like the Germans use. Maybe we should gather some pine cones. We could tie them on the branches if there's nothing else."

Daniel began to look around for the prickly cones.

"Let's cut lots of extra pine boughs too," she suggested. "Pauline wants to make Christmas wreaths. And let's see if we can find some of that California holly."

They dragged the tree down the hill to the wagon. As they began to load it, Daniel spotted another good straight pine. "Let's cut that tree too."

"Two Christmas trees?" Suzannah asked as if he had taken leave of his senses.

"One for the house, and one for the deck of the *Bostonia*, to remind the miners that it's almost Christmas."

She shook her head, her brown braids swinging from under her red cap. "Decorations will get ruined in the rain."

"Then we'll use weather-proof decorations—pine cones, acorns, and such," Daniel decided. "Captain Scully has a sailmaker cutting awnings from the ship's sails for the main deck. We could put the Christmas tree under one near the gangway."

"Well, we can't say that Daniel Meriwether Colton doesn't come up with good ideas once in awhile." Suzannah admitted. "And I've got another one. We can make stars and angels from straw in the barn—" She put out a hand to feel the first cold drops falling from the leaden skies above. "Now let's collect those pine cones and get home before we drown in this rain!"

The scent of pine filled the parlor, bringing back all kinds of wonderful memories of Christmas back home in Virginia—caroling around the little pump organ while Mother played, baking Christmas cookies, hiding home-made presents in the attic to be proudly displayed on Christmas morning. . . . Now here they were clear across the country, making a new home for themselves . . . and new memories. At least Daniel had all the people he loved most with him, not like Suzannah, who had lost both her mother and father in that steamship explosion. He resolved to be more thoughtful and stop teasing her so much . . . at least until after Christmas!

Mother gave him a searching look, then broke into his thoughts. "Do you have nuts, raisins, and dried fruits in the ship's store, Daniel? Your Aunt Pearl and I hope to make Christmas fruitcakes."

"I'll look tomorrow," he promised. "If there's any to be found in the town of San Francisco, I'll find them. You know how much I like fruitcake!"

"That I do, Son!" Mother laughed. "And we'll need sugar and flour and molasses and honey—"

"It would be nice to string popcorn for the tree too," Aunt Pearl put in. "I've heard that makes a nice decoration, and . . . land sakes, Ruth, we'd better make a list if we expect Daniel to remember everything!"

"There's thin wire in the barn," Uncle Karl said. "Garth and I can make hangers for yer ornaments. Guess we'd best make plenty since you got a tree for the *Bostonia's* deck too."

After Karl and Garth left for the barn, Pauline let out a sigh. "I hope, in spite of everything, that we can invite Charles for Christmas dinner," she said.

Mother and Father exchanged a long look, then Mother gave a little shrug. "Well, dear, if it would make you happy, of course we'll invite him. We wouldn't be so hard-hearted as to keep a man from his own family at Christmastime."

"And who knows? Since his . . . business . . . hasn't worked out to his satisfaction, Charles may be ready to come home and be a real husband and father," Father added encouragingly.

Pauline gave them a grateful smile. "I've written him a letter," she confessed hesitantly. "Would you deliver it, Daniel? I'm afraid to do it myself, afraid he might turn me down—"

Daniel glanced at his father, who nodded. "I'll do it." But he, too, dreaded the thought of facing Charles again.

Pauline brought the letter out to him. "You're so good to do this, Daniel."

"I'm not good at all," he protested. He had a thousand shortcomings—and avoiding Charles Herrington was at the top of the list. Still, he'd promised Pauline and he'd follow through . . . tomorrow.

By evening, the tree was dressed in acorns, pine cones, red calico bows, and golden straw angels. Adorning the top-most bough was a great straw star Pauline had made. Lighted candles, nestled in wreaths of California holly and placed around the parlor, cast a mellow glow over the room.

Daniel put another log on the fire in the fireplace and watched the flames dance higher. The house no longer seemed quite so strange; in fact, it was beginning to feel downright homey.

———◆◆◆———

The next morning, before they rode off to work at the ren-ovated ship, Father spoke to all of them. "We'll be reminded of the robbery as soon as we see the old brig, but we have to put it behind us. We'll take precautions now, like pulling in the gangplank as soon as the last customers leave. We can only hope it will never happen again."

They arrived at the Boston Brig Emporium before the first customers appeared. A white canvas awning already flapped over the section of deck where the cashier would collect receipts. None too soon either, for heavy dark clouds sent sheets of rain slashing down, and Daniel and the others had to run for cover.

Refusing to let the dreary weather dampen his mood, Daniel hurried down the steps to the 'tween deck, ignoring the passageway to the captain's cabin and heading straight for the store they had set up there—the 'Tween-Decks Shop, as they had decided to call it.

Moving behind the counter, Daniel began to gather some of the items on Mother's list. He packaged sugar and flour, and found cans of molasses and honey. No nuts, raisins, popcorn, or candied fruit for the fruitcakes though. He'd have to find those elsewhere.

Working side by side with Father through the morning, Daniel jotted down additional items they would be needing to replenish supplies. This list was like many a stock list he had made for the store in Georgetown.

About midmorning, Daniel climbed the steps to the main deck. There, under a canvas awning near the gangway, was the tall tree they had cut earlier, now bedecked in Christmas finery. Two miners were helping Ned add the last few pine cones and straw ornaments.

"Ain't never seed a Christmas tree," one of them said in a reverent tone. "But I heerd tell the King of England puts 'em up in his castle."

"Then you must come see the one in our home too," Father suggested. "We'd be pleased if you'd come to our Christmas service and stay for supper afterwards."

"Maybe we will!" said the other miner.

When Daniel returned to the 'Tween-Decks Shop, through the open hatch, he could see Karl and Garth working with Captain Scully in the cargo hold below. They were prying open crates containing furniture, farm tools, and other heavy items. Before long, they'd all be familiar with the stock of the Boston Brig Emporium!

As Daniel looked on with interest from his vantage point above, Uncle Karl ripped off a section of crate, revealing an instrument of polished rosewood.

"An organ!" Uncle Karl exclaimed. "A pump organ! Where'd that come from?"

"Supposed to deliver it from Boston to missionaries in the Sandwich Islands," Captain Scully replied. "But I'm afeard dampness has already gotten the better of it."

Calling for Father and the others to join them, Daniel rushed down into the hold to view the treasure. As they carefully removed the crate, they found a small rosewood pump organ and matching bench, still in fine condition.

Sliding onto the bench, Father began to pump the pedals. There was a whoosh of musty air, then a wheeze. But after the initial complaints, when Father tried the keys, the sweet tones filled the cargo hold. "It sounds fine. Wouldn't this be just the thing for our Christmas Eve service? Ruthie used to play the organ at church, and I believe Pearl did too. They grew up in a musical family, you know," he added, nodding to Daniel.

"Pearl sorely misses her music," Uncle Karl said, stroking the fine polished wood. "Wish we could buy it for 'em somehow."

"Well, why don't you take it home for now?" Captain Scully suggested. " 'Twould be better off in your parlor where there's heat than here in this cold, damp hold."

Daniel turned wondering eyes on the captain. "Wouldn't they be surprised? What a Christmas present!"

At noon, the rain stopped, and more miners slogged through the mud toward the Emporium. By now, however, the planking laid down for a front walk to the gangway had nearly disappeared in the mud.

"Me an' Garth'll break up more crates, but we're near out o' wood," Uncle Karl said with a frown. "There's a half-sunk barge carryin' lumber stranded out there in that mess o' ships. Most likely, they'd be glad to get rid of it at a low price before they go down. After lunch, we'll row out the longboat."

An idea struck Daniel. "If Ned can tend the 'Tween-Decks Shop, I'd like to take the dinghy out to see about finding the rest of the things on Mother's list. If you'll give me some gold dust, maybe I can buy Christmas provisions for the store too. There's an English ship out there, and, if it's like the ones that sailed into Georgetown, they may have tinned sugar biscuits and cakes."

"While you're at it, son, maybe you can scout out what the other ships are carrying. With new ships sailing in every week, I wouldn't be surprised if there are enough supplies to stock our store for some time."

Early in the afternoon, Daniel dragged the dinghy to the water's edge.

"See that you don't get yerself shanghaied!" Uncle Karl yelled after him. "I figger there's many a captain out there who'd be glad to get together enough sailors to set sail for another port."

Daniel waved to his uncle in reply. He'd heard of ship's captains who kidnapped boys and men, then forced them to work aboard their ships, often putting out to sea and not returning for years. He intended to be careful.

He pulled the dinghy into the water and rowed out to the jumble of abandoned ships, their naked masts rising from the water like skeletons. Stopping by a half-sunken vessel named the *Kanaka Trader*, he yelled, "Ahoy! Anyone aboard?"

A bewhiskered captain stuck his head over the brig's railing. "Just a few o' us, sonny. Most o' the crew took off for the gold fields, but I'm hopin' to get a new crew together now that it's rainin'. If you run across any good sailors tired of diggin' for gold, send 'em up to me . . . no questions asked."

Daniel decided that if the captain had been planning to shanghai anyone, he wouldn't have spoken about getting a crew together. "I'll tell any I see," he called back.

"There were some South Sea Islanders out at the diggings." He hesitated, then asked, "You got anything aboard for a Christmas dinner? Nuts, dried fruits, popcorn, and such?"

"Christmas!" the captain repeated. "Almost forgot. There's kegs of dried pineapple molderin' in the hold and burlap sacks of nuts. Probably all rotten by now. But come take a look-see yourself."

He dropped the rope ladder down the ship's side, and Daniel tied up the dinghy. Before the captain could change his mind, Daniel started up the swaying rope ladder.

"You got fam'ly in this town?" the captain asked as Daniel stepped onto the deck.

"Yes, sir. I live with my mother, father, cousins, and all," he replied. "We were headed for Oregon by covered wagon, then changed course when we heard about the gold."

"Not surprised to hear it," the captain said. "Gold fever's as catchin' as the pox, and purt nigh as deadly too. Well, come on down to the hold. I'd like a real fam'ly to have what ain't rotted."

Daniel remembered Uncle Karl's warning about being shanghaied, but this captain seemed harmless enough. He followed him down the steps to the cargo hold.

The captain opened a keg of dried pineapple that was still good, then a sack of fine unshelled walnuts. "Take 'em, sonny. They're yours."

After thanking him, Daniel eyed a huge crate of half-rotten sweet potatoes. "Would you sell those too?"

"He'p yourself," the captain answered. "It's a gift fer yer family. A Christmas present from the *Kanaka Trader*."

Daniel thanked him again. "We own that old ship that's been beached ashore," he explained, pointing out the Boston brig in the distance. "We're turning it into a store for the miners. Maybe we can sell some of these things, but I couldn't take much in the dinghy—"

"Then come back fer more, sonny. Better to give it to you than to have rottin' cargo, drawin' rats."

Daniel slanted a look at the captain. "Y-you wouldn't shanghai a boy, would you?" he asked hesitantly.

The captain chuckled. "Is that what's been worryin' you?"

"A little," Daniel confessed.

"Well, it never hurts to be careful with strangers. But to tell you true, most of these ships out here can't move an inch, either because their hulls has rotted out, or because they need a full crew to move 'em out to sea."

Daniel breathed a sigh of relief. When he climbed back into his loaded dinghy, he called back, "I'll tell sailors you're looking for a crew. Merry Christmas, Captain! And God bless you!"

"And you, sonny!" the captain answered. "When you're ready fer more, come back. I fear I'll still be here!"

As Daniel rowed the dinghy toward the shore, he could see Father waiting with a wheeled cart. Jumping out in the shallow water near the beach, Daniel hailed him and together they pulled the dinghy ashore and tied it to a piling near the water's edge.

"Well, I'll be!" exclaimed Father when he saw the sacks and barrels of produce.

"Sweet potatoes and dried pineapple," Daniel said, helping to unload them. "Walnuts too. The captain of the *Kanaka Trader* gave it to us and said to come back for more. In exchange, he'd like us to send him any sailors who want to go back to sea."

Father shook his head in amazement. "You drive a good bargain, Son! That's the best deal I've heard! I know the tent restaurants would be glad to buy sweet potatoes for a change too. Had a fellow in this morning who was buying crockery and tinware to start up his new place and was looking for some food items we didn't have."

They worked in silence for a few minutes, hoisting the barrels into the cart and shifting the sacks for better balance.

After they'd unloaded the dinghy, there was still plenty of daylight for another buying trip. "Thought I'd try a Yankee clipper for the popcorn and raisins," Daniel told his father.

"Just keep your wits about you, Son."

Daniel nodded, but he felt much better about the whole thing since the captain of the *Kanaka Trader* had told him that most of the abandoned ships in the bay were unable to put out to sea, even if they shanghaied a crew! Heading out with the dinghy again, he spent all afternoon rowing from one ship to another. If the vessel was occupied and the captain seemed honest, Daniel climbed up the rope ladder and bought supplies from him. If there was no one in sight or if the captain looked suspicious, he simply made up some excuse and shoved off for the next ship.

It was nearly dark when Daniel returned to shore with the loaded dinghy. This time the boat held tins of English biscuits and cakes as well as sacks of raisins, popcorn, brown sugar, and Virginia hams.

"I used all the gold dust you gave me," Daniel confessed when his father met him with the wheeled cart.

"Never mind, Son. These goods are worth twenty times what you paid for them. I don't know how long we can get such bargains, but for now we'll have the least expensive goods in San Francisco. We'd better make you our chief buyer!"

"I wouldn't mind," Daniel replied. "I like rowing out and meeting the sea captains. Most of the men stuck out there are glad to hear news from shore. What happened while I was gone?"

"The miners bought out our stock of tinned biscuits and candies. Seems they got the Christmas spirit when they saw our tree on the main deck. They're remembering Christmas back home, I imagine, so many of them seemed pleased when I invited them to our Christmas service."

"Think they'll come?"

Father shrugged. "Some of them may be there."

By the time Daniel got back to the ship, he saw that Uncle Karl and Garth had laid down planks over the crate-wood around the brig to form a makeshift street, and the sailmaker had added an awning over the midsection of the main deck.

The place still looked more like a ship than it did a store though.

Down in the 'Tween-Decks Shop, his uncle and step-cousin were helping Ned wait on miners. It had been a busy day, they told him. Daniel was equally pleased with his success in bringing in provisions. All in all, they were making progress with their new lives in San Francisco. It wasn't until they rode home that he remembered: He hadn't delivered Pauline's letter to Charles!

———————◆◆———————

The next morning Daniel and his father drove the wagon into town to bring home the organ. The morning fog hung thick and white, and the tents and crude buildings looked like shadowy ghosts. In fact, it was almost impossible to make out what were now familiar landmarks.

Daniel peered through the mist. "Where's Charles's gambling tent supposed to be?"

"Some of the miners told me it was just around the corner from Portsmouth Square," Father said, leading the oxen carefully along the rutted road. "His fundraising must have gone well. He's hired carpenters to build a wooden gambling palace behind the tent, so I'm told."

Daniel let out a discouraged sigh. "Hear anything about him cheating?"

"They didn't mention it. They did say, though, that he serves the best drinks in town and sometimes food too, when he can get it."

"Guess I'd better invite him for Christmas Eve soon," Daniel said. "Pauline asked me about it again last night." He walked on in silence, then muttered under his breath. "I don't see why she wants him around, though, when he treats her so mean!"

Before long, the two were so busy loading the organ into the wagon and bracing it for the trip home that Daniel put Charles and his business dealings out of his mind.

That evening, when the organ was installed in the parlor and Mother settled on the little bench to finger the first soft chords, it was easy to forget all about the man who seemed less and less like a member of the family.

Jamie clapped his hands when he heard the music, and baby Annie's rosebud mouth turned up in a smile of delight. But Suzannah, sitting next to Daniel, grouched under her breath, "Daniel Meriwether Colton, you get *all* the excitement!"

"What a joy to have music in the house again," Mother said, not hearing Suzannah's complaint. "Isn't the Lord good to provide an instrument just in time for Christmas?" She began a familiar melody.

When the sweet strains of "Home Sweet Home" ended, Daniel was ready for more. "Play some Christmas carols like we used to sing back home, Mother."

Her fingers moved over the keys, searching out a tune before settling into a beloved hymn, "O Come, All Ye Faithful." One by one, the voices took up the melody, then blended in harmony— Mother's husky contralto, Uncle Karl's and Father's rumbling bass, Daniel's clear tenor, and Pauline's and Suzannah's pure sweet soprano, rising above the others.

When the last note faded, there was a long pause while each recalled memories of Christmases past.

"Maybe we oughta start our Christmas Eve service with that one," Big Red said. "It's one most folks know."

"Pearl, you really should play," Mother suggested. "I feel so out of practice, and you always were the better organist.

Yes, you definitely should play for the Christmas Eve service."

"Oh, Ruthie!" Aunt Pearl protested. But Mother insisted, and Aunt Pearl seemed pleased as she sat down at the organ. "I'll have to practice," she said and swept into a lively tune that set their toes to tapping and lifted their spirits, before slowing the tempo and striking the tender chords of "Silent Night."

Looking at all the dear faces gathered around the organ, Daniel felt a lump lodge in his throat. This was his family and he loved them all . . . well, *almost* all of them. He still wished he could feel differently toward Uncle Karl and Cousin Garth. At least he knew them a little better. He could sympathize with their bitterness, could even partly understand how hard it was to forgive the Indians who had killed Uncle Karl's wife and Garth's mother.

He knew they needed the gift God gave the world at Christmas so long ago. They needed Jesus. Daniel hoped they would receive that gift before it was too late—

———————◆◆◆———————

For the next two days, Daniel was busier than ever, selling food and other goods to the tent restaurants, and buying more provisions from the abandoned ships.

"You've got a real eye for business, Son," his father complimented him. "All it really takes is finding out what people need and supplying it. Maybe God means for you to be a merchant like me."

"Maybe," Daniel replied. What *did* God want from him? It seemed he'd been praying about it for ages, at least ever since Ned Taylor's baptism back along the trail. Now Daniel was really confused. He didn't know if he wanted to be a sailor, climbing high into the riggings of great sailing ships

. . . a seaside merchant like Father, selling the world's goods . . . or a minister, telling the wonderful news of God's love.

Passing through Portsmouth Square again, he looked at the bearded men wandering in and out of the noisy saloons and gambling tents. Many were drunk and aimless. Instead of being disgusted though, he felt sorry for them. What he really wanted was to tell them how to find joy, but studying to be a preacher at a seminary back East would be expensive.

When he returned home, Suzannah asked, "Have you invited Charles yet?"

"Tomorrow," he promised.

"Want me to do it?" She wrinkled her nose and cocked her head. "I wouldn't mind some excitement."

"I'll do it tomorrow." Yet whenever he passed the Herrington Palace, Daniel felt like running in the other direction. Tomorrow he'd ask God for courage.

The next morning, Daniel stayed busy waiting on customers at the Boston Brig Emporium. No sense in trying to see Charles before noon, because he usually gambled until late at night and slept all morning.

By midday, Daniel had run out of excuses. Slowly he loaded the wagon and got ready to leave for the short trip over to the center of town. "I'm taking the rest of the sweet potatoes and hams to the tent restaurants," he told his father. "I'll stop by Charles's place first."

"I'll keep you in prayer," Father said.

As the wagon rolled out, Daniel was suddenly fearful. Uttering a prayer for help, a Scripture verse came to mind: "Perfect love casteth out fear," and he repeated it over and over as they neared the Herrington Palace. In front of the big tent, he halted the oxen. Carpenters were busy hammering together a wooden building behind the tent, and a new plank sidewalk led to the tent entrance, where a gigantic bronze-skinned guard eyed him with suspicion.

Daniel nodded, Pauline's letter in hand. It would be easier to give the letter to the guard, but he'd promised Pauline that he would deliver it in person.

The guard, massive arms folded, watched his every move. "Make delivery at back," he said tersely.

"No delivery. I'm Charles Herrington's cousin by marriage. I need to talk to him. I was wondering if you'd watch my wagon."

"I Kao," the guard replied.

"Are you from the *Kanaka Trader?*" Daniel asked, thinking there was something familiar about the man.

"Maybe yes, maybe no."

"The captain needs some more good sailors for an ocean voyage, if you're interested."

The man threw back his head and laughed, revealing strong white teeth in a smooth-shaven tanned face. "Me no more sailor. Me work for Charles Herrington."

"Well, then, I'll look for him myself."

"His room in back," Kao said. "I take you."

Daniel started into the noisy tent, amazed to see so many miners already at the gaming tables. The smell of cigar smoke and the stench of hard drink filled the air, and on the right, a long bar stretched half the length of the tent. Leaning against the bar, two drunken sailors sang loudly, "Mussels and mussels and mussels and clams!"

Just then Charles stepped into the room. His dark hair was slicked back, and he was wearing his fine black St. Louis suit, a diamond stickpin in his necktie. His gaze swept the tent and stopped to rest on the sailors. Clenching his jaw, he strode angrily through the crowded room, another giant of a man right behind him.

Daniel's mouth dropped open! Charles's bodyguard seemed the image of the guard at the front door, the one who was escorting him through the tent at this very moment. He gulped and turned to see if his eyes were deceiving him.

"Is Kio, my twin brother," Kao explained.

Daniel had a peculiar feeling that he'd seen them before. Something about them was so familiar. On the other hand, most South Sea islanders spoke in broken English.

As the sailors boomed forth their rowdy song, Charles ordered, "Throw them out! This is a gambling palace, not a saloon for drifters and drunken sailors!"

Kao and Kio hustled the sailors out, half-carrying them by their collars.

Turning away, Charles caught sight of Daniel. "What are *you* doing here?"

Daniel felt everyone's eyes on him, and for an instant, he felt about six years old. He swallowed hard. "I-I'm here to deliver this letter from Pauline, inviting you to our house on Christmas Eve." Right now, he'd give anything if Suzannah were here instead of him!

Charles glared at him for a moment. "Let's go to my office." He turned to the crowd. "Get back to your gambling. This is a private matter."

Charles led the way to a smaller tent inside the large gambling tent, and opened the flap. Inside, a black lacquered Chinese desk held papers, pen and an inkwell, while a bright red screen adorned with Chinese carvings was arranged to give privacy to Charles's living area.

Closing the flap behind them, the tall man took a seat behind the desk and motioned to Daniel to sit down in the chair opposite him. "Sorry I was so abrupt out there. How can I help you?"

Daniel sat, his mouth open. *Charles Herrington* apologizing? He almost forgot what he had come to say. "Pauline wanted you to have this." He handed Charles the letter, then waited for him to open it.

After reading the letter, Charles refolded it and put on a pleasant smile. "Well now, rumor has it that you've become quite the young businessman, quite the businessman indeed." He tapped his fingers on the desk. "Maybe we can do a little business . . . together," he added. "What treasures have you found in the bay lately?"

"Sweet potatoes and Virginia hams—"

"I'll buy the hams," Charles interrupted. "How many do you have?"

"Twenty. But I'm taking them to the tent restaurants."

Charles closed his eyes in thought, then opened them and rose to his feet. "I'll pay double what they'd give you."

Daniel opened his mouth to object, but Charles said, "Four times!"

"Four times?" Daniel gasped.

Disappearing behind the screen for a moment, Charles called to Daniel, "Did you actually promise the hams to anyone?"

"No, but—"

Charles stepped from behind the screen and handed Daniel a pouch. "This gold dust is worth five times what you'd get for your hams anywhere else in town."

Daniel's resolve wavered. Maybe selling to Charles just one time wouldn't be wrong. Maybe it would even put him in a good mood about accepting Pauline's invitation. A man ought to be with his family at Christmas.

"I understand you're a fine supplier," Charles went on, sitting again at his desk and placing his fingertips together. "I'd like to contract you to find me the best food and drink in town. Needless to say, I'll pay you well."

Daniel set the pouch on the desk. "I'm sorry. We don't sell hard drink. As for selling you food . . . I'd have to ask Father and Captain Scully."

Charles leaned back, put his booted feet on the desk, and regarded Daniel through slitted eyes. When he spoke, his voice was pitched low and oily-smooth. "No. This is between the two of us . . . men. You bring me hard drink, and I'll guarantee you enough money to set yourself up in a business of your own."

Daniel took a deep breath and straightened his spine. "I'm sorry. I can't do that."

The tight little smile curved Charles's lips once more. "Then . . . for now . . . I'll settle for food only."

For a moment the thought lingered in Daniel's mind, tempting him. *Just think what you could do with all that money. Father and Mother wouldn't have to work so hard. Pauline wouldn't need to feel bad about not paying her way at home. Maybe, too, this would give you a chance to be a good influence on Charles, maybe even lead him to Christ like you did Ned Taylor!*

"Are you coming to the house on Christmas Eve?" Daniel asked.

Charles's lips narrowed into a thin line. "*If* you'll agree to supply food for my place. It wouldn't be stealing from your precious Emporium, if that's why you're so worried. You can pay them off to the penny, and still have plenty left over for yourself."

Daniel thought of Pauline and gave in. "Food only," he finally answered in a small voice. "And half of my profits go to Pauline."

Charles stood up behind his desk and offered his hand. "Let's shake on it then. I trust you, Daniel, which is more than I can say for most of my own employees. That's why I have to stay here, as you've probably guessed."

His explanation sounded believable, Daniel decided. The arrangement could always be ended if Charles didn't live up to his part of the bargain. Besides, this handshake might lead to a whole new life for Pauline's husband. Slowly, tentatively, Daniel reached out to shake Charles Herrington's hand.

CHAPTER 6

"Daniel Meriwether Colton!" Suzannah exclaimed. "You talked me into helping you decorate your presents, and you're not even listening to me!" She gazed at him across the dining room table, scissors and a half cutout calico wreath in hand. "What's wrong anyhow?"

He didn't look up. Instead he glued the first green cotton wreath to a white-wrapped tin of hard candy. The house was fragrant with the scent of pine and the aroma of fruitcakes baking in the oven, just like it should be the week of Christmas. Everything was fine, except . . . "Charles!" he exploded at last. "Charles is what's wrong!"

Suzannah plunked down the scissors. "What's he done now?"

"Shhh! Not so loud."

He glanced at the oak door leading to the kitchen. It was closed, but Pauline was in there, glazing fruitcakes with Mother. In the parlor Father, Aunt Pearl, and Big Red were planning the Christmas Eve service, and out in the barn,

Ned, Garth, and Uncle Karl were building benches in case of an overflow crowd.

Daniel eyed Suzannah thoughtfully. "You won't tell?"

"I won't tell," she promised.

"*If* Charles comes, it's mainly because I agreed to supply him with food for his gambling tent."

"Daniel! You didn't!"

He squirmed. "It seemed right at the time. He wanted me to sell him hard drink too, but I flat-out refused to do it."

"Well, I'm glad to hear that at least!" She narrowed her blue-green eyes in thought. "So *that's* how you got the gold for Pauline!"

He nodded. "I sold him some hams. Twenty of them."

"I'd gladly bong him over the head with one of those hams, the way he treats my sister. And not for a minute do I believe he's so busy he can't stay here with her and the children."

"He says he has to keep an eye on the people working in his gambling tent," Daniel explained. "There've been robberies all over town. Anyhow, I'm sorry I told you, but I had to get it out."

She gave him a long look. "To tell the truth, I'd have probably done the same thing if I was in your shoes. I'd do just about anything to make my sister happy. And nothing could make her happier than to have Charles home for Christmas!"

Daniel straightened. "*If* he comes. Once I'd sold him the hams, he suddenly wasn't so sure he'd come, after all."

"Wouldn't that be just like Charles?" she snorted in disgust. "Where do you suppose he got the money to buy that big tent and the gambling tables and everything else?"

"I figure he got someone to lend him the money to get started, and now he's on a winning streak. He did the same thing in Alexandria."

"Let's hope it doesn't turn out the same here," she said. "What did you tell Pauline?"

"I just couldn't tell her the whole truth, so I told her he'd probably come."

"Did you tell your father about selling Charles those hams?"

Daniel shook his head. "No. Between moving in here and the store just opening, Father's got plenty on his mind."

There was a long silence while Suzannah and Daniel continued to wrap packages. "Well," she said at last, "in spite of everything he's done, I'm still praying for Charles."

"Me too. I'm praying this Christmas that he'll turn his life over to Christ instead of letting gambling be his god."

Christmas Eve morning, the Boston Brig Emporium was busier than ever. Miners and tent restaurant owners bought up all of the sugar, flour, nuts, sweet potatoes, and every last tin of sugar biscuits and cakes.

"We close up at one," Daniel told the customers as he packaged the goods they had bought, "but we're having a service tonight at our house. You're welcome to come and stay for supper afterwards."

"Thank ye kindly," said one of the miners. "We might do that."

Daniel gave them directions to the house.

"Wait 'til you see who's coming tonight," Father called over with a wide grin.

"Who?"

Father laughed, his green eyes dancing. "Wait and see."

Riding home in the wagon, Daniel prayed, *Please, Lord, let Charles come tonight. Send Thy Holy Spirit to soften his heart.*

At the house, Lad and Lass ran out to greet him, barking and wagging their tails. "Come on out to the barn with me," he told them, leading the way. "You'll be spending the night here. Can't have you jumping all over our guests."

When he hurried back to the courtyard, he saw one of Pauline's pine wreaths, tied with a red calico bow, hanging on the entry gate. Inside the house, Aunt Pearl was practicing "Angels, from the Realms of Glory" on the organ, and his heart pounded with excitement.

Suzannah raced out the door to meet him. "What happened in town today?"

"Nothing new," he assured her. "We just stayed plenty busy."

At dusk, they hung lanterns at the gate and in the courtyard, bathing the house and grounds in a golden glow. Soon after, Daniel and his family were dressed in their new clothes. Even little Jamie and baby Annie were wearing new garments that Pauline had lovingly sewn for the occasion.

In the parlor four rows of benches placed in front of the horsehair sofa and parlor chairs would provide plenty of seating. They faced the pump organ and fireplace, where a cheery fire blazed.

At the sound of horses and wagons rolling up outside, Father said, "Let's greet them and make sure there's enough light out at the hitching post."

Daniel noticed that Uncle Karl and Garth hung back when he and the others rushed outside to welcome the visitors.

"Ahoy, there!"

"It's Captain Scully!" Daniel told Ned.

Riding with the captain were two of the men who had helped to ground the *Bostonia*. And behind them came four miners on horseback. "Good of ye to think of us," one called out. "Yeah! 'Specially the invite for supper!" said another.

Father laughed and introduced everyone. "If you'll take these gentlemen in and make them feel at home, I'll stay out here to greet new arrivals," he told Daniel and Ned.

Captain Scully looked around the courtyard. "Fine place you have here . . . for landlubbers, that is!" he said, bringing on a round of hearty laughter.

"Mother and Aunt Pearl can't wait to thank you for the use of the organ," Daniel said. "And wait until you see that stove in the middle of the kitchen. It's Mother's favorite thing in all of California!"

Mother and Aunt Pearl beamed at the captain when Daniel introduced them, then confessed about their masquerade in the covered wagon the day the *Bostonia* sailed ashore. "We just couldn't bear to miss such a sight," they admitted.

"Well, I'll be!" the captain declared. "You're right adventuresome women."

"Not usually that adventuresome," Aunt Pearl said. "It was Suzannah's idea."

The captain smiled. "Should have knowed. Took her to be a gal with spunk first time I laid eyes on her."

Tonight, when Daniel had first seen Suzannah in her new blue dress and her braids tied up in matching ribbons, she almost looked like a lady. But when she grinned and her eyes sparkled with mischief, he was relieved to see that she was the same old Suzannah.

By the time they'd given their guests a tour of the house, more men had arrived for the Christmas Eve service. Pauline and Suzannah served coffee while Jamie watched the growing crowd with wide eyes, and baby Annie gurgled and cooed in her cradle.

"Good to be in a real home again," one miner said, taking off his hat and looking around with awe.

"I don't mind sayin' I'm lookin' forward to hearin' the Good Book read too," said another crusty miner. "Don't rightly know how long it's been since I've been inside a church."

Father seemed pleased to hear it. "At the rate San Francisco is growing, we'll need churches soon."

Just then, Big Red ushered in a man Suzannah recognized right away. "Mordechai!" she squealed.

Daniel turned in surprise, then hurried to greet the white-bearded mountain man who'd led them from Missouri to California. "Didn't know you were coming!"

Mordechai gave a laugh. "Didn't know it meself till I heard in town you folks was havin' a worship service 'n' supper. Best news I've heerd since the first gold strike!"

Everyone greeted their old guide happily.

"Come sit up front with Suzannah and me," Daniel said. "I'm in charge of keeping logs on the fire."

"Ye always was a good hand at that," Mordechai said, following them to the front row. Instead of his greasy buckskins, he was wearing a brand-new blue flannel shirt, corduroy pants, and tall black boots.

"You look like a real miner," Daniel said.

"Ain't givin' away me buckskins though," Mordechai replied, rubbing his chin through his scrawny white beard.

"If I find enough gold, I aim to buy me a ranch up in the mountains."

At that moment Daniel felt an unusual prickling sensation, as if someone's eyes were boring into his back. Turning, he saw Garth on the fringes of the crowd, not yet mingling with the others and looking resentful about the whole event.

"Garth!" he called to his stepcousin. "Come say hello to Mordechai."

Mordechai stood to shake hands with Garth, then patted him on the shoulder. "Ain't you the fine gen'leman, dressed up in a suit?"

Garth shrugged, not quite hiding his pleasure.

Warmed by the steaming coffee and good conversation, the men gradually drifted into the parlor and found seats, filling the benches and spilling over onto the sofa and straight-backed chairs. While Daniel stoked the fire once more, Suzannah handed out papers on which she had written the words to several carols. Aunt Pearl took her place at the organ and began to play softly, waiting for the rustle of the papers to subside.

Almost every seat was taken, Daniel noticed as he sat down again between Mordechai and Garth. But as far as he could tell, Charles was still missing. There was Pauline in the back row, saving a place for him near the parlor door.

Presently Father stepped to the front and stood before the crackling fire. "Welcome to all of you this Christmas Eve. We're leaving the gate open in the hope that others might still join us. Octavius Brooks—you may know him as Big Red—will lead our worship, and my dear sister-in-law, Mrs. Karl Stengler, will play the organ. We hope you'll sing out and make this a Christmas to remember as we celebrate the birth of our Savior."

At the back, Daniel heard Pauline murmur, "Charles!" Turning, he saw the tall man slide onto the bench next to her and Jamie. Charles nodded as people looked at him. He looked the picture of a devoted family man.

Hopeful, Daniel turned back to face the front of the room.

Big Red had stepped forward, looking fine in his black suit. He opened the big family Bible and began to read: "And it came to pass in those days, that there went out a decree from Caesar Augustus, that all the world should be taxed. . . ." The familiar story of Joseph and Mary and their trip to Bethlehem unfolded as the big man read on: "And she brought forth her firstborn son, and wrapped him in swaddlin' clothes, and laid him in a manger; because there was no room for them in the inn."

Big Red's deep voice brought the scene to life: "And there were in the same country shepherds abidin' in the field, keepin' watch over their flock by night. And, lo, the angel of the Lord came upon them, and the glory of the Lord shone round about them: and they were sore afraid."

Daniel closed his eyes, imagining what it must have been like to see angels in the middle of a dark night. He'd have been scared too!

"And the angel said unto them, Fear not: for, behold, I bring you good tidin's of great joy, which shall be to all people. For unto you is born this day in the city of David a Saviour, which is Christ the Lord. And this shall be a sign unto you; Ye shall find the babe wrapped in swaddlin' clothes, lyin' in a manger.

"And suddenly there was with the angel a multitude of the heavenly host praisin' God, and sayin', Glory to God in the highest, and on earth peace, good will toward men."

Daniel opened his eyes, and Big Red was smiling at them. "Let's stand together and sing 'Angels, from the Realms of Glory.' "

Aunt Pearl played the "Come and Worship" chorus as they stood, then Daniel sang out with the others about angels winging their flight over all the earth to proclaim Messiah's birth. Darting a glance at Garth, he was surprised to see his cousin actually joining in. But he wasn't surprised to see a tear rolling down Mordechai's wrinkled cheek. For all the old mountain man's bluff and bluster, Daniel had learned that he was really gentle, almost a believer—

When they all sat down again, a hush hung over the little group.

"We sing those words with such joy every Yuletide, then most of us forget 'em for the rest of the year," Big Red said. "Some because they don't have Christ in their hearts.

"Think on this now, friends, if you only remember Jesus Christ at Christmas, he's likely not your Savior and Lord. Oh, I feel such a call upon me to ask you to think on it. Christ said, 'I am the way, the truth, and the life: no man cometh unto the Father, but by me.' Will you accept the gift God gave on the first Christmas? It's the best one you'll ever receive."

Daniel prayed harder for Charles.

Big Red smiled with expectation. "If there's somebody who feels the Lord callin' and wants us to know it, just come on up."

He waited while the room grew so still one could hear the flames popping on the hearth and the creak of the pine flooring underfoot. Daniel felt movement on either side of him, and cracked an eye open.

Mordechai took a step forward, then fell on his knees . . . and Garth right behind him. Then a rugged-looking miner made his way from the back of the parlor, tears rolling down his cheeks.

"Anybody else want to step up here for Christ?" Big Red invited.

No one else moved.

Charles! Daniel prayed. But Charles stayed in his seat. Big Red smiled. "It was on a Christmas Eve like this when I first stepped out for Christ too. And it's been a grand adventure ever since to walk along the trail with Him, and have His Holy Spirit to guide me." He bowed his head and led a prayer for Garth, Mordechai, and the miner. Finishing, he added, "There may be somebody else who wants to pray this prayer in his heart. If you do, just say, 'Heav'nly Father, forgive me for my sins and wash me clean through the blood of Thy son, Christ Jesus, who was sent to be my Savior and Lord.' "

Daniel hoped as hard as he could that Charles was praying along with them, but he didn't dare look back. After a while, when Mordechai and Garth returned to the bench, Daniel couldn't help beaming at them. When everyone stood and sang "Joy to the World," it seemed to Daniel that the light of the Lord shimmered all around them, that in these holy moments, the darkness had fled.

At the last "Amen," people crowded around Garth, Mordechai, and the miner. Daniel shook Garth's hand.

Garth's voice was hoarse with tears he tried to hold back. "Now I *want* to forgive 'em. . . . I want to forgive them Injuns like you told me."

Daniel's eyes clouded too. He saw Mother take his aunt's place at the organ, and Aunt Pearl rushed over to hug Garth. "I've been praying and praying for you, . . . Son. I'm just so happy that you had the courage to come forward."

"Onct I took the first step," Garth said, "all the others was easy."

After Mother played "God Rest Ye Merry, Gentlemen" twice, Father stepped to the front again. "What a Christmas Eve to remember," he said. "Despite all of the lawlessness around us, God still comes to those who open their hearts to receive Him. Let's give thanks to Him again and thanks for the supper ahead."

When it was over, Daniel headed for the back of the parlor and overheard Charles in a heated argument with Pauline. "I can't take the whole night off," he was saying. "I thought you'd be glad I could make the service, but I guess there's no pleasing you, is there?"

Pauline's eyes brimmed with tears, and Charles turned to Daniel. "Come by my place tomorrow."

"But tomorrow is Christmas Day," Daniel protested.

"I'll expect you . . . tomorrow!" Charles repeated firmly. There was no mistaking the finality in his tone.

CHAPTER 7

On Christmas morning, there was leftover ham with eggs and pancakes for breakfast, and Mother declared, "Never in my life have I seen so many hungry men as after that service last night!"

Father laughed. "It appears that hunger for God doesn't dull hunger for good cooking. What's more, some of the men are coming back Sunday to discuss holding regular church services."

Daniel glanced over the dining room table at Garth. His stepcousin's face still glowed with quiet joy. "Glad you made the decision?"

"Yep," Garth replied simply. "Big Red says God has a plan for me. Imagine that. . . . God lovin' a feller like *me* and givin' me a plan. Wonder what could it be?" He paused a moment. "Well, all I really know is that I feel like a dif'rent person."

"You even *look* like a different person," Suzannah said. "Not so mean and grouchy. Just wait and see! Now your life will be an adventure every day!"

Garth looked over at his stepmother. "I didn't guess you was prayin' for me. Reckoned nobody really cared 'bout me after my ma died . . ."

"Oh, someone cared about you, all right," Aunt Pearl assured him. "Lots of folks, for that matter. I wasn't the *only* one praying for you."

Uncle Karl gave her a small smile. "You prayin' for me too, Pearl?"

"I am," she admitted. "Praying for the people I love is as natural to me as breathing."

Uncle Karl looked down at his plate. "Guess I should've expected it, marryin' a church-goin' woman."

Daniel chuckled along with the others, glad Uncle Karl had taken it so well. The Christmas Eve service seemed to have made a difference for everyone except Charles. He couldn't help wondering what Charles would have to say when he failed to show up at the gambling tent as he had ordered.

"What a lot of miracles we've had here already," Big Red said. "Findin' this house, startin' a new business in an old brig, and our first Christmas service bein' such a wonder. We have lots to be thankful for this mornin'."

Ned Taylor had been strangely quiet during breakfast, though he'd put away his share of pancakes, Daniel noticed. Now he spoke up. "I miss my brothers and sisters back home," he said, "but we never celebrated the real meanin' of Christmas the way you folks do. Guess this is the best Christmas I ever had."

Daniel looked around the table at all the happy faces. He was about to say, "That goes for all of us," until Pauline entered the room with a fresh batch of pancakes from the kitchen. She looked so woebegone that he hadn't the heart to say anything else. For Pauline, it was not the best Christmas ever. Charles wasn't here—

Breakfast continued without further comment. When they had all finished, Father rose and pushed his chair back under the table. "Let's open those presents under the tree. In honor of your decision for Christ last night, Garth, how about you and Ned handing out the presents?"

He laughed as the two boys made a dash into the parlor. The others followed, settling on the horsehair sofa and a couple of the new benches.

"Never saw so many presents!" Garth remarked as he looked at the circle of gaily wrapped packages spilling out from under the tree.

"After almost a year on the way here, everything we had was worn out," Mother explained. "We can't look like ragamuffins forever."

Garth read the first tag, "For Ruthie Sunshine," and handed it to Mother.

Her blue eyes danced as she gazed up at Father.

"Open it," he encouraged.

She untied the red bow, then unfolded the white paper with care. "Why, Franklin! Blue calico fabric! Enough for a dress!"

"To match your eyes," Father said.

She gave his cheek a fond pat.

"Shoes!" Suzannah exclaimed, opening a large package. "Guess you were afraid I'd start wearing my Indian moccasins again."

"They smell so bad, they've already walked out by themselves!" Daniel teased.

She stuck out her tongue at him, and he grinned and reached for his first present—a pair of boots like the miners wore. Next came a blue flannel shirt, then a belt and socks. When he looked around the parlor again, he saw lots of new clothes and yard goods, which made his tins of candy especially welcome when they were opened.

"Wagon!" Jamie crowed, showing everyone the wooden toy Big Red had made for him. "Wagon!"

"How very kind of you," Pauline murmured, but there was a sadness in her eyes. Probably wishing Charles had been the one to make something for his son, Daniel thought.

"My pleasure, ma'am. I like to see the children happy," Big Red replied shyly.

Charles hadn't brought by a single gift for her or the children, Daniel realized with a flash of anger.

As if reading his mind, Pauline spoke up, "Charles sent along his present early . . . some money he gave Daniel for us . . . but we're receiving so many presents, we won't need to buy much at all."

Daniel thought she sounded a little too cheerful and bright, and her determined smile began to slip and soon disappeared altogether.

It was the money he had earned from Charles! Daniel drew a deep breath. Well, it had bought Pauline a little happiness, so maybe he'd done the right thing by giving it to her and telling her Charles had sent it.

He picked up another package with odd lumps and bumps beneath the white tissue wrap. "To Daniel, from Uncle Karl," he read on the tag. Surprised, he looked up, but his stepuncle pretended not to be watching.

Daniel untied the red string, then unfolded the paper. Inside was the carefully carved likeness of an ox that he recognized immediately—Marigold! "Thank you, Uncle Karl! It's mighty handsome."

His uncle gave a nod. "Made it for you 'cause you turned out to be handy on the covered wagon trek, after all. It took plenty of doin', but you proved me wrong."

Daniel felt his ears grow warm. His freckles were probably standing out like copper pennies too. But he didn't care. A compliment from Uncle Karl about his frontiering days was almost better than a carved ox—

It rained hard all day Sunday, and only a few miners rode out to the worship service and stayed afterward to talk about starting a church. The rain didn't dampen their spirits though, for they all felt the same: Without more godly people in San Francisco, evil would grow stronger yet.

On Monday morning, the rain was still pouring when Daniel rode into town with the other menfolk. The horses' hooves kicked up mud, spattering his pants and boots. When they passed near Charles's gambling tent, Daniel felt a chill that was not altogether the fault of the weather. Charles was probably pretty mad at him for not obeying his order to report to his tent. He would be madder still when he learned that Daniel had decided never to work for him again.

At the Boston Brig Emporium, they saw the second layer of crate-wood walkway sinking into the mud. "If it keeps raining like this," Father jested, "our horses will mire up halfway to China."

By now, everyone was so wet they didn't even smile.

"Ahoy, mates!" Captain Scully called out from beneath the white canvas canopy. "Didn't know if you'd be comin' in this weather!"

"A little rain won't stop us," Daniel answered.

"A *little* rain?" the captain repeated. "This is just the beginnin', lad. We've got at least two or three more months of the Californy rainy season ahead."

"We'll have to lay more crate-wood on the walk," Father said. "On the other hand, the rain might discourage our customers."

"You'd be s'prised," said Captain Scully. "Even on Christmas Day and Sunday, the miners milled all about with nothin' to do. In bad weather, they want to be inside, and most don't care if it's a store or a gamblin' tent. I told the sailmaker to use all the sails he needs to make an awnin' big enough to cover the main deck."

Before long miners and tent restaurant owners arrived, looking for food, boots, dry clothes, and India rubber ponchos. Most of all though, they wanted something to eat.

"We've run out of food," Daniel had to tell them. "But we'll be getting new supplies just as soon as the storm lets up."

"Expect we could butcher some cattle tomorrow," Uncle Karl said. "Them restaurant owners would be glad to buy beef, if nothin' else."

When Daniel went up to the main deck later in the morning, he squinted through rain at the abandoned ships in the bay. Strong gusts of wind buffeted the vessels this way and that, causing them to crash into each other. Tall masts splintered and toppled to the decks, tangling what was left of once-white sails in a snarl of ropes. Soon the ships would be beyond salvaging, and Daniel knew the few men aboard would be looking for another ship or even for dry land beneath their feet. He would have to act fast to buy up the last of the cargos. But the waves were far too choppy today to make the trip.

"Don't know how we'll buy food and supplies if this storm doesn't break," he said.

"Let's open every last crate in the hold and make sure of what's there," Big Red said. "I've got a feelin'—"

"Stoves," Captain Scully said with confidence. "You're welcome to open 'em, but for the most part, all you're goin' to find is more cookstoves."

"Let's try anyway," Garth said to Daniel. "I'm not much good at sellin' boots and raingear to miners anyhow."

Down in the ship's hold, the two boys climbed over the merchandise to reach the row of unopened crates. Hanging a lantern on a peg, they used crowbars to pry open the last six crates.

Stoves, more shiny black stoves, just as Captain Scully had predicted.

When they cracked open the last crate, Daniel's disappointment was obvious. "Another stove." But as they pulled it aside, he saw something that sent his hopes rising. "There are three more barrels up here!" he called out. "We must've overlooked them!"

Pulling the crate wood aside, they climbed into the very back of the hold. When Daniel saw the lettering on the barrels, he laughed. "Pickles. Three barrels of pickles. But won't Suzannah be glad? She likes pickles."

"I wouldn't mind having pickles with that beef we brought from home," Garth said. "Just the thought of it has my mouth waterin'."

They rolled the barrels to the bottom of the steps and heard Father call down, "Daniel, there's someone here to see you. He'll meet you on the 'tween deck."

Who could that be? Daniel wondered. He hurried up the steps and found a very large man standing beside the counter. He was wearing a rubber poncho, his broad back turned to Daniel. "You . . . uh . . . wanted to see me?"

The man turned. One of the South Sea islanders from Charles's place!

"Yes?" Daniel asked uneasily.

"Have letter," the man replied. It took a moment before he remembered to reach under his poncho and bring out the envelope. "You read . . . answer now."

Daniel accepted the letter uneasily. DANIEL COLTON, PERSONAL, it read. Recognizing Charles's handwriting on the envelope, he tore it open and unfolded the sheet of white paper. Charles's message was short:

> *Need to buy food from you. Kao will pay you. Get out*
> *to the Russian ship that came in yesterday. They*
> *might have caviar and such.*
>
> *Charles*

Daniel crunched the paper in his fist, his temper rising. The nerve of that man! Not that barking out orders, or writing them, for that matter, was anything new for him. As Daniel stood there, thinking, Kao loomed over him like a mountain in his huge black poncho.

Daniel looked up at his dour face. "We don't have any food left except three barrels of pickles—"

The man nodded. "Take pickles . . . all barrels."

"But we have to be fair. The miners and tent restaurant owners want to buy food from us too."

"All barrels," Kao insisted.

"*One* barrel." Daniel was determined not to let Charles get away with this. "And tell Charles not to send anyone again. I'm not doing any more business with him."

Kao slapped a pouch of gold dust on the counter. "Charles Herrington, he no like. One barrel now. Come back for more."

"It won't do you any good to come back. I won't sell you any more."

Kao raised his dark brows. "We see. Where barrel?"

"Down in the hold." He watched as the huge man lumbered down the steps and returned, shouldering the barrel with ease.

"Charles Herrington, he no like," Kao warned again.

"No more business," Daniel repeated firmly, heading for the counter. He slipped the pouch of gold dust into his pants pocket. He'd pay the Emporium with half the gold dust and give the other half to Pauline. He wouldn't keep even a pinch for himself.

Nervous, he straightened the piles of receipts and order sheets. Before long, he saw Big Red and Garth struggling to carry another barrel of pickles up the steps. "I'll give you a hand," Daniel offered.

As they wrestled it up onto the main deck, everyone was staring at Kao, who was carrying his barrel out into the rain as if it were no more than a loaf of bread.

"Wouldn't want to tangle with that brute," said one of the miners.

"Did he pay you, Daniel?" Father asked. "He claimed he did and acted downright surly when I asked about it."

"He paid," Daniel answered. "More than enough too. I'll bring it up. Meanwhile, we've got two more barrels of pickles. Here's one of them."

"Pickles?" a miner exclaimed. "Guess it's better'n nothin'. Even with ships comin' in to port, there's not much to eat in town now. Guess we'll live on pickles 'til the rain stops."

Daniel felt his father's eyes resting on him. For an instant, he was tempted to confess what he'd done, but Father would . . . well, he'd probably say he should have told him in the first place. Anyhow, Daniel decided, he was over thirteen years old now, and he'd gotten out of the mess by himself. Did he always have to tell his parents everything?

CHAPTER 8

Torrents of rain fell all day, and Uncle Karl, Ned, and Garth rode home early to butcher five of their cattle for food for the miners. By the time Daniel arrived, the smell of roasting beef filled the house. As long as there were thousands of cattle in California, no one would starve to death, he decided.

The next morning, he and Garth rode to town in the covered wagon to deliver the beef to the tent restaurants. The horses' hooves made soft sucking sounds as they pulled their legs from the mud, spattering it on their underbellies.

Garth peered out through the driving rain. "There's Charles's gambling tent."

Daniel spotted a familiar sight—one of the giant South Sea islanders standing guard at the entrance to the tent. Daniel hunkered down so as not to be seen. As they rode on, he mused, "Wonder how Charles is feeding the gamblers? He's bound to have run out of food by now, which means they'll have to eat somewhere else, maybe in someone else's gambling tent. He'll lose business, and that will make him plenty mad." The thought was not a pleasant one.

By noon, they'd finished making their deliveries and drove the wagon back to the brig. Garth stared out at the rain. "I don't care now about goin' back to them gold hills when the rains stop. Be just as glad to work on the ranch. Don't know, but . . . since I accepted Christ . . . I ain't so all-fired restless."

Daniel grinned. "That's because you've got peace in your heart now."

Garth nodded. "Yep. Guess that's what it is. Pa's still itchin' to go out to the gold diggin's come spring."

"I wouldn't mind hunting gold for a day or two," Daniel admitted, "but I wouldn't want to build my whole life around it."

On the fourth day after Christmas, the rain slackened down to a drizzle. Daniel, Ned, Garth, and Big Red rowed out into the bay in the ship's longboat. At the *Kanaka Trader*, the captain was glad to see Daniel again. He seemed grateful too, for the beef and fruitcakes Mother and Father had sent along as gifts.

"Best pay I've had in a long time," he said.

"This time we're paying in gold dust for the goods," Daniel insisted.

A short time later, they loaded the longboat with kegs, barrels, and crates of sugar, salt pork, dried pineapple, and the last of the sweet potatoes.

As they left, the captain jerked a thumb back toward the ships riding low in the water behind them. "Expect that brig just in from Chile would be loaded with vegetables . . . potatoes, onions, peppers, carrots, and beans. And that British ship stopped in China. So they're apt to have baskets, floor mattin', lacquered furniture, and such."

When Daniel thanked him, the captain said, "Glad to be useful. You'll go far, lad. just keep your wits about ye."

Hmmm, Daniel thought. Father had said the same thing.

They spent the rest of the afternoon visiting the newly arrived ships and arranging to transport the cargo to shore. Now they'd have a good supply of food to store in the 'Tween-Decks Shop.

It was still raining when Daniel set out alone for home in the covered wagon. In the downpour, the two lanterns hanging in front shed only small circles of light on the road ahead. One moment, the horses were slogging along through the rain and mud, and the next, someone was shouting, "Stop! Stop or we shoot!"

Daniel's heart thudded, and he reined in the horses hard. "Whoa, boys! Whoa!"

Two riders approached, wheeling their horses as they pulled up. In the lantern light, Daniel could see their broad brimmed black hats worn low, red kerchiefs over their faces, and the silvery glint of two guns aimed directly at him.

But the garb they were wearing did not disguise one man's broad shoulders and erect bearing nor the other's huge bulk, as they sat in their saddles. *Charles . . . and one of his South Sea Islanders!*

"I know who you are," Daniel blurted, then wished he'd held his tongue.

"Figured you would," Charles said, "but this way you can claim you were stopped by 'masked men.' " He tossed a canvas bag at Daniel. "Take this and buy caviar and vodka. There's enough gold dust in that bag to buy plenty and pay you handsome profits as well."

"Why won't you believe me?" Daniel pleaded. "I can't sell you any hard drink."

Charles ignored him. "Turn that wagon around and drive it behind my tent. Kao will make sure you do what I say. I'll need a good many kegs of caviar and several barrels of vodka. Buy as many as the longboat will hold."

"I told Kao I'm through buying for you."

"No one backs out on me," Charles said, his voice hard and cold. "If you value your home and your family . . . you'll do it."

Daniel eyed Charles's gun. "You'd threaten *your own family?*"

"Call it what you like!" Charles snapped.

It took Daniel a moment to recover from his shock. "But why do you want *me* to do it?"

Charles studied him from behind the mask. "Because you can be trusted. The captains give you better prices than a grown man can get. Some of them even seem to want to *give* it away."

"You're wrong! Only one captain ever gave me anything. We pay now, like everyone else. Why don't you use your guards to do your dirty work?"

"If they weren't so dumb, I would."

Daniel glanced at Kao, who seemed unaware of the insult.

"They are loyal, however," Charles went on. "I'm convinced they'd be loyal to the end, which is more than I can say about my own family."

"That's not fair," Daniel protested.

Charles's eyes narrowed, done with the subject. "Take out half of that gold dust and hide it in the wagon for Pauline and yourself. Carry the other half out to the ship." With that, he wheeled his horse and rode off into the rainy darkness.

Daniel shivered, certain Charles would carry out his threat. Finally, he opened the canvas bag. It held smaller pouches. Kao was watching. So, heartsick, Daniel followed Charles's instructions. Just a few days ago, he'd spoken of becoming a preacher, and now he'd be buying hard drink for a gambling tent. After tonight, God probably wouldn't want to have anything to do with him.

"Turn wagon," Kao grunted.

Daniel turned the horses back toward town, shivering in his poncho. He wouldn't be missed for a long time because Father and the others were still working at the store. *Lord, please help me,* he prayed, but no answer came.

At last, they pulled up behind Charles's soggy gambling tent. The moment the horses halted, Kao hustled Daniel out of the wagon. "We go to Russian ship now."

"We can't row a longboat . . . not just the two of us," Daniel objected. "Especially not when it's loaded with goods."

"Kio and Russian sailors go with us," Kao said. He shouted something into the tent, and his brother came out carrying a lantern, followed by two other men. Together, they pulled a longboat from under a nearby canvas.

They dragged the longboat through the rain toward the water, then pushed off and jumped in. "You hold lantern," Kao told Daniel, thrusting it at him. "We row."

Despite the rain, the sailors navigated skillfully through the thick tangle of ships anchored in the bay. Daniel wondered if the two Russians had deserted the brig. Shortly, they pulled up alongside.

"You call," Kao told Daniel.

Daniel obeyed reluctantly. "Ahoy there! Ahoy!"

When someone with a lantern peered over the railing and answered in a foreign language, Daniel called back, "I want to buy caviar and . . . and . . . vodka!"

"Caviar? Vodka?"

The two sailors in the longboat yelled up in what must have been Russian. It sounded like some kind of explanation. Then haggling over prices began. Too soon for Daniel, the men on deck dropped down a rope ladder.

"You go up," Kao ordered. "Show man gold. Tell him 'No more.' *Nyet!*"

"Me?" Daniel asked, stalling for time as long as he dared.

"You!" Kao threatened.

Daniel hung the canvas bag around his neck, twisting it around back so it was under his poncho. Wiping the rain from his face, he scrambled up the rope ladder, holding on for dear life as the wind whipped him about.

Tell me what to do, Lord, he prayed.

No answer came.

He climbed over the railing onto the ship. Sailors were already rolling kegs and barrels along the deck. The captain blinked in surprise to see a boy, but Daniel did as he was told, holding open the bag for the captain's inspection and repeating the Russian word over and over. To his astonishment, the captain finally nodded in agreement. Maybe what Charles had said was true: A boy might do better than a man at some things.

Why hadn't the Lord stopped him? Half expecting to hear thunder from heaven, Daniel motioned for the kegs and barrels to be loaded into the longboat below.

Then, suddenly, he knew the answer. *Since God gives every person freedom of choice, Charles has chosen evil,* Daniel thought, *and he's tangled up his own family in its web! Still, God is greater than evil.* A Scripture verse came to mind: *And we know that all things work together for good to them that love God, to them who are the called according to his purpose.*

Daniel didn't see how it was possible, but he hoped that somehow something good might come of all this.

When he returned home, everyone pounced on him.

"Where have you been?" Suzannah asked. "What happened?"

Daniel was sorely tempted to tell until he remembered Charles's threat. "I was waylaid on the way home . . . on the edge of town." He hoped he sounded convincing.

Father was furious. "Highwaymen!"

"Are you hurt?" Mother asked.

"Only wet and cold," Daniel replied, pulling off his dripping poncho.

Suzannah rolled her eyes, exasperated. "You have all the fun and excitement! What did they look like? Did they wear masks?"

"Just kerchiefs over their faces, and black hats."

"Did they steal anythin'?" Garth wanted to know.

Daniel shivered. "Only my time. There wasn't anything much in the wagon."

"We'd just decided to ride back into town to see if we could find you," Father said. "Now I wish we had. I'd like to get my hands on those hoodlums!"

"You'd have only gotten wet," Daniel answered, shivering harder. He felt a sneeze rising and turned his head just in time. "Achoo!"

"Quick, change into some dry clothes," Mother fussed. "We'll get some hot soup in you before you catch your death of cold, and then get you right to bed."

Daniel was grateful to escape before they quizzed him further, especially Suzannah who was always full of questions.

Later while he ate hot beef soup in the kitchen, the men discussed the problem of lawlessness all around. To his surprise, no one asked if he knew the identity of the hold-up men. He ate his soup in silence, listening.

"We have to do something about these criminals," Father insisted. "It's getting so decent folk can't be out in safety. And with so many new gold seekers coming in every day, it's bound to worsen."

Especially if they're like Charles, Daniel thought. By the time he finished his second bowl of soup, he was feeling warmer. But his shivers didn't subside completely until long after he was in bed.

The next day, Kao clumped down to the 'Tween-Decks Shop to buy tins of crackers and other supplies. When he paid, he handed Daniel a note that read, "Meet me at dark behind my tent." The note was unsigned, but he recognized the handwriting.

Daniel nodded miserably. Tonight was New Year's Eve. No doubt Charles meant to start the new year by fleecing as many drunken gamblers as possible.

After darkness fell, they returned to the Russian ship for more caviar and vodka. "Charles Herrington, he say we do this two times a week, maybe more," Kao told him. "Go to other ships when they come in. You watch."

We'll see about that, Daniel thought, then recalled Charles's threats. Maybe if he'd told Father everything from the beginning, it wouldn't have come to this.

Trading with the Russian ship went quickly this time, and he ran the horses hard all the way home to keep his family from worrying. Since everyone's mind was on the New Year's Eve supper, he was scarcely missed.

As the weeks passed, only Suzannah eyed him with suspicion. But when it appeared that she was on the verge of asking a question about his trading trips, Daniel always managed to change the subject, or he'd tweak her braids, then run like the wind.

Besides, Charles had arranged everything. While Daniel bought goods for the Emporium, he ordered for Charles, as well. Then, either the captains delivered Charles's supplies by longboat, or Charles sent his own men to collect them. And since Daniel made most of his buying trips alone, no one at home was the wiser.

Rain fell endlessly throughout January and February. The streets were so muddy that people claimed a good-sized horse had been sucked under.

When a committee of citizens came to buy all of the remaining stoves in the hold, Captain Scully was puzzled. "All of them?"

"As many as we can get to sink into the streets for a foundation," one replied. "That mud's a danger for man and beast."

Captain Scully turned to Father. "We've got six stoves left. What say we donate one to the cause and sell the rest to this committee here?"

"If you agree, I believe we should do it," Father replied. "I'm in favor of improving the town in any way possible."

Daniel watched as the cookstoves were submerged into the muddy streets. As the week passed, the heavy cast-iron stoves settled lower and lower into the mud. It reminded him of how he'd been slowly sucked into working for Charles Herrington.

Despite the rain, ship after ship sailed into the bay, and thousands of gold seekers streamed into San Francisco. It was all Daniel could do to buy enough goods for the Emporium—and food and drink to be delivered to the Herrington Palace.

Every day, he watched through a spyglass for incoming ships, then set out to meet them in the longboat. It was a great adventure to visit ships from all over the world, then to sell their goods in the 'Tween-Decks Shop. But he hated his work for Charles, whose new gambling palace was nearly complete.

Count your blessings, Daniel reminded himself grimly. One of these was hearing Captain Scully ring the ship's bell each morning when he opened the brig, calling out a cheery, "All hands, ahoy! The Boston Brig Emporium now open for business!" And each evening hearing his "Ahoy, all hands! Closing time! All ashore!"

With a little effort, he could even find a few blessings in working for Charles. He seldom saw Charles, but next time he did, he intended to tell him about Christ once and for all. And, thanks to their agreement, Pauline now had money for her share of the household upkeep. Since Charles rarely visited, the money helped her feel loved.

Last of all, Daniel had been able to save a good bit of the gold dust he'd earned from trading. He still hoped to go to seminary someday and learn how to be a real preacher. That is, if God had any use for him now!

CHAPTER 9

By mid-March, about twenty miners were attending the Colton worship services in the parlor every Sunday morning. On Sunday afternoons, Daniel went in to town with Big Red, who held services for a crowd of men on Portsmouth Square.

It was on one of these Sunday afternoons, as Big Red spoke in the heart of the gambling district, that the sun at long last broke through the rain clouds. The bystanders blinked at the unaccustomed light and rubbed their eyes. *Lord,* Daniel prayed, *shine through the darkness in these men's hearts just like the sun.*

"Christ said, 'I am the way, the truth, and the life: no man cometh unto the Father, but by me,' " Big Red told the crowd. "And I say, Now is the time for salvation. This may be your last chance to make a decision for Christ."

Daniel saw a few hardened faces soften and a few tears roll down grizzled cheeks. He hoped that Charles might come from the nearby Herrington Palace to hear, and just then his wish was granted, for Charles stepped through its swinging doors. He wore his fine black riverboat gambler suit and appeared surprised, then angry at the scene before him.

At least a hundred miners began to sing "The Royal Proclamation," and Daniel sang out with all of his might, hoping the words would stir Charles's hard heart:

Hear the royal proclamation,
  the glad tidings of salvation
published now to every creature,
  to the ruined sons of nature.
Lo, He reigns, He reigns victorious
  over Heaven and earth, most glorious,
Jesus reigns!

Daring to turn his head, Daniel glanced at the spot where Charles had been standing. Gone! Charles was gone. As usual, he couldn't bear to hear the truth about God.

After Big Red's last "Amen," he spoke with the miners who'd come forward to accept Christ. *Now,* Daniel thought, knowing he couldn't put it off any longer. *Now is my chance to speak with Charles.* He hurried through the crowd to the Herrington Palace. When he reached the swinging doors, he sent up a prayer and, for the first time, stepped inside the wooden building.

A man was pounding out jangly music on an upright piano, and the room before Daniel's eyes was nothing like the dirt-floored gambling tent. In fact, he had never seen anything like it in his entire life! Rich red draperies, fringed in gold, hung at the windows. The oak floor was covered with thick Chinese rugs, and polished oak gleamed around green felt gaming tables. Over the bar an ornate mirror, framed in gold, reflected the elaborate chandeliers, which by night, would be twinkling with dozens of lighted candles. Yet for all the costly furnishings, the gamblers themselves hadn't changed a bit, Daniel noticed, for the stench of cigar smoke clouded the air, and several of the players were cursing over a disappointing turn of the cards.

At the bar, Kao struggled to subdue an unruly miner, and a few customers glanced Daniel's way. "Where's Charles Herrington?" he asked them.

"Back in his office," one replied. "Say, ain't you a mite young to be in here?" He guffawed at his own joke. "Not that it matters hereabouts."

"Ain't you the boy with the preacher?" asked another of the men at the bar.

Daniel nodded, then dodged through the knot of curious customers who had drifted over to stare at him. A round of coarse laughter followed him, and it seemed to take forever to make his way through the raucous place. Finally, in back, he came to a polished oak door on which gold letters spelled out the word *PRIVATE*. He hesitated, took a deep breath, then knocked.

From within, Charles growled, "Who's there?"

"Daniel. Daniel Colton."

After a long moment, Charles spoke in a more pleasant voice, "Come in."

Daniel opened the door, feeling like the Daniel of old when he was thrown into the lion's den.

Inside, though, the office didn't look like a lion's den. Fine wood paneling covered the walls, and Charles himself was sitting behind his black lacquered desk. "Well, well, if it isn't the preacher's sidekick." His lips curved upward, but his eyes glittered with suspicion.

Daniel forced a smile himself. "That's . . . what I've come to talk about." He hadn't really planned what he would say, but now the words came with conviction. "There's robbing and killing all over the territory, Charles, and some of it's because of places like this. What people need isn't gambling and drink, what they need is Christ—"

"Don't you preach to me!" Charles yelled, rising to his feet.

Daniel remembered the softened hearts when Big Red had spoken in the square. Plucking up his courage, he persisted, "I've always backed down about this before, but not now. There's only one way to be happy and that's knowing God."

"Enough!" Charles exploded. "Get out of here!"

Daniel paused. "Well, then at least I need to tell you I won't be working for you anymore. It's time I told Father what I've been doing, like I should have from the beginning. I dreamed up some high-minded excuses so I'd feel better about it, but that's all over."

Charles glared at him. "I told you . . . *no* one backs out of a business arrangement with me."

"Guess I'll be the first," Daniel replied. He turned to leave. There had been no sign of a gun, but a spot between his shoulder blades burned as if expecting to feel a bullet at any minute. He headed out, not looking again at Charles until just before the door closed.

Charles's face boiled with fury. "I'm not through with you yet, Daniel Colton!"

All the way home, Daniel thought of his encounter with Charles, but he didn't want to spoil Big Red's joy over the miners who'd given their hearts to God. Besides, Father should be the first to hear that he'd been working with Charles.

When they arrived home, supper was ready. Afterwards, Father went out to the parlor with Big Red for a private discussion, and Daniel resigned himself to waiting longer.

"Think I'll go out to the courtyard now that it's stopped raining," Suzannah said. "If the storm clears, there should be a full moon tonight."

"Be sure to wear a wrap," Mother called out to her.

Suzannah rolled her eyes, but grabbed her cloak from the rack by the parlor door.

"Maybe you shouldn't go out—" Daniel began.

"Why not?" Suzannah asked, indignant. "*You* get to go to town and out to the ships by yourself, but I'm always stuck at home. I'm getting sick and tired of it too!"

A sudden chill crept down his spine. Charles had threatened the whole family, and now that Daniel had walked out on their business arrangement, there was no telling *what* he would do. "Then I'll go with you."

"You don't have to."

But he tugged on his jacket and followed Suzannah out to the courtyard anyway, closing the parlor door behind them.

Soft light shining from the lamps in the windows fell on the red-tiled veranda. The entry gate was always locked at nightfall and, except for the dripping of the bushes and huge pepper trees, there was not a sound to disturb the stillness.

Suzannah gave him a curious look. "Why didn't you want me to come out here alone?"

Daniel looked up at the clouds scudding across the face of the moon. The courtyard seemed safe enough now, but he'd have to tell her, to warn all of them. "Because Charles has been making threats."

"Threats . . . about what?"

"Against our family . . . if I don't do what he says. He wants me to buy—"

A huge hand clamped over his mouth and a strong arm pulled him off his feet. At that moment he saw another dark form grab Suzannah, but she managed to let out a small squawk before her voice was muffled.

Daniel struggled, kicking hard.

"Stop . . . or you be sorry!" Kao snarled.

The next thing Daniel knew, a gag covered his mouth and was knotted hard behind his head. Moaning, he tried to kick Kao again, only to have the giant's fist slam into his chin. Daniel sagged in pain.

"Move!" Charles ordered. "And stay out of the light!"

Charles! Daniel thought, amazed that he would actually come to the house.

Jaw aching, he was half pushed, half carried through the courtyard shadows to the front gate. Someone had cut the lock, for Charles simply took it off and shoved him and Suzannah out onto the road, then pulled the gate in place behind them.

From the direction of the barn, Lad and Lass barked two or three times, then fell quiet. If only he could whistle for them—but no! Even if he didn't have a gag in his mouth, the dogs had been put up for the night, and unless someone let them out, they wouldn't be able to track his whereabouts.

Once they were out of hearing range, Charles muttered to the guards, "Get these brats into the wagon and tie them up. I'll ride ahead. Kao, you drive."

Daniel and Suzannah were shoved roughly into the wagon, then tied with ropes as Charles had instructed. When they'd finished, Daniel lay in the covered wagon, feeling as helpless as a rabbit trussed up over a cookfire spit. He heard Charles ride away, then heard Kao sit down on the driver's seat. Kio settled inside by the tailgate to watch them.

Kao flicked the reins over the horses, and the wagon lurched forward. Daniel glanced at Suzannah in the moonlight. Like him, she lay on her back, arms tied behind her, legs bound at the knees and ankles. Probably she was miserable too. Was Charles just trying to scare them? Daniel wondered as they bounced along in the wagon. Or would he actually do them harm?

As they rode, Daniel bit on the gag over his mouth, hoping to ease it off, but it was too tight. As for loosening the ropes that cut into his wrists, that seemed impossible. *Lord, we need your help!*

The trip seemed to be taking forever. Where were they going? Did their family realize they were missing? Daniel wondered. Probably not. Everyone felt the courtyard was safe, and the outer windows of the house were shuttered because of the rain. He imagined Mother and Father. . . . No, he couldn't bear to think of them now. More important to watch for a chance to escape.

After a long while, the shrill sounds of piano music and off-key singing filtered through the wagon's canvas top and grated on their ears. They must be nearing the saloons and gambling establishments of San Francisco.

"Whoa!" Kao called out, and pulled the wagon to an abrupt halt.

As Kio climbed down, Daniel guessed they were behind the new Herrington Palace. A man approached the wagon with a lantern. Maybe someone was coming to help them! But Daniel's hopes were dashed when he recognized Charles's voice.

"Wrap those tarps around them, then, take them in through the back door of my office. And make sure no one sees you. We'll deal with them later."

Daniel felt himself wrapped and rolled up like a rug, surrounded by darkness. Kao and Kio grunted as they carried him into Charles's office. After dumping him on the floor, they clomped out and returned with Suzannah, who moaned fiercely.

"Leave them here," Charles said. "They won't be going anywhere, but I'll lock the door just in case."

Daniel listened as Charles turned the key, then walked briskly down the hallway. Here on the floor the tinny sounds of the piano seemed louder, and someone let out an oath, followed by coarse laughter.

Rolled up like a mummy, Daniel could barely breathe. He edged over onto his side to ease the pain in his shoulders and arms. Getting loose was still doubtful, although he was working his head out of the tarp. Where was Suzannah? From her moans, he only knew she was somewhere nearby on the floor.

Heavy footsteps neared the door, and a man's voice rasped, "Herrington! You in there?"

Daniel and Suzannah moaned again through their gags, but the man couldn't hear them, for he muttered under his breath, "Ought to do the town a favor and get rid o' him. He's cheatin' the other miners out o' their gold too."

"Ummmmmmm!" Daniel moaned.

"Expect he's gone out to eat supper," came another voice. "We can come back later. Got to find 'im when them two giants ain't standin' guard."

Their steps slowly faded as the men walked back toward the laughter and loud music.

Twisting and turning his head, Daniel bit at the gag again. He hadn't even been able to work a small hole in it. Finally, he stopped to rest. Time passed slowly, and he tried to imagine Mother and Father deciding what to do when they realized he and Suzannah were missing. Likely Father would look for clues, and after a while, he'd see the broken lock on the entry gate. Mother's blue eyes would fill with tears. Pauline would . . . well, it would break her heart if she guessed Charles's part in it. Uncle Karl would be angry, as usual.

After what seemed like hours, he heard a key turning in the lock, then Charles's voice. "Take them to that old ship I told you about. It'll sink any day now, and we'll be rid of them for good."

Surely Charles is only trying to scare us, Daniel thought in horror, *just so I'll agree to work for him again. And by kidnapping Suzannah too, he thinks I'll give in.*

Daniel tensed every muscle as he felt himself being lifted and carried out to the wagon behind the gambling house. The men looking for Charles hadn't returned yet, either. If only they would come now.

Kao and Kio deposited Daniel in the back of the wagon like sacks of potatoes. Minutes later, Suzannah was roughly dropped beside him.

"Make sure you're not seen, whatever you do—" Charles warned the guards.

"Herrington!" a loud voice interrupted.

Daniel was certain it was the same man who'd pounded on the office door, the one who'd said, "Ought to do the town a favor and get rid o' him."

"Yes?" Charles replied carefully, looking around. "What do you want?"

"You've pulled your last cheatin' trick—"

"Stop him!" Charles shouted. "He's got a gun!"

There were shouts, then the sounds of a mighty scuffle near the wagon. A barrel or some other heavy object hit one of the wagon wheels, jostling the wagon against the horses' flanks.

Suddenly there was gunfire. "Aaayyy!" came an awful cry of pain.

Who had been shot? Charles? His pursuers?

"He got me—" rasped one of the two men. "But I killed that cheatin' gambler. He. . . won't . . . live to cheat . . . no more."

Charles! Daniel thought. In the wagon, he lay stiff with fear as men scurried about in the darkness. If he could just roll himself over the side.

"We go!" Kao said to someone, probably Kio. "We do what Mist' Herrington say."

No! Daniel thought. Surely Kao and Kio weren't that dumb . . . or that loyal to Charles! Their employer was dead . . . or was he?

"Giddap!" Kao yelled. The horses moved forward, drawing the wagon jerkily behind them. "Giddap!"

The horses ran faster and faster. When at last Daniel heard the sound of waves in the distance, his throat tightened. If, as Charles had said, Kao and Kio were loyal to the end, and if they meant to put him and Suzannah on an abandoned ship . . . The prospect was so frightening, he dared not think about it!

Inside the covered wagon, Daniel twisted and tugged to get free, but succeeded only in causing the ropes to cut deeper into his flesh. Still, if he could work his wrists loose, then release Suzannah—

Too late! Kao was slowing the horses and pulling the wagon to a stop. The strong pungent smell of the sea blew across his face, and the sound of waves washing against the shore filled the night. What was going to happen next?

"Out . . . here," Kao ordered.

"Ummmmm!" Daniel moaned, hoping they would remove the gag from his mouth. If he could just try to reason with them, maybe even offer them the gold dust. "Ummmmm!"

"Ummmmm!" Suzannah echoed.

"Quiet!" Kao rasped.

Wispy clouds drifted across the moon while the guards dragged Daniel from the wagon. Despite the darkness, it didn't take long to see what Charles had planned for them.

The men dumped Daniel into a longboat near the water's edge, then shoved Suzannah in beside him. As the clouds moved on, the two of them looked like ghosts in the moonlit night.

Kao and Kio pushed the longboat into the water, then jumped in and began to row furiously. A spray of water flew up, drenching Daniel's face and the gag on his mouth. The salty water burned his sore jaw, but he hoped that the moisture would loosen the cloth.

"Ummmmmmm!" he moaned over and over, but his groanings were lost in the sounds of the oars scraping against the sides of the boat.

As they rowed out into San Francisco Bay, Daniel felt certain that he and Suzannah must be missed at home by now. Maybe Father, Big Red, and Uncle Karl were already in town looking for them. He craned his neck to see if another boat had followed them.

There was nothing but the moonlight rippling across the surface of the sea.

Before long, the graveyard of half-sunken ships came into view, and Daniel worked harder to loosen the gag from his mouth. As he sawed at the cloth with his teeth, the masts of the tilting ships reminded him far too much of silvery skeletons.

"There!" Kao pointed toward a ship listing to the stern. "Soon, she take more 'n more water. Then, goodbye, ship . . . goodbye, brats!" He laughed loudly, and when the big man ran his finger across his throat, Daniel knew he was not joking.

"Ummmmmmmm!" Daniel pleaded, hoping the men would take pity on them now.

Kao cast him a heartless glance. "Charles Herrington, he pay us plenty to do job . . . we do it."

Well, so much for his idea of bribing the twins to set them free. Daniel shook his head. "Ummmm!"

"Quiet!" the brothers answered, tying up the longboat. "Quiet, or we be madder!"

Looking around, Daniel noticed the ship's rope ladder hanging down the side, doubtless left there when the ship was abandoned. He considered throwing himself overboard, but wrapped in the tarp, he wouldn't have a chance in the cold water. Even if Charles had only meant to scare him into submission, the guards were taking his orders seriously. But surely God didn't want his and Suzannah's lives to end here.

Kao lifted Suzannah to his shoulder as easily as he'd lifted the pickle barrel in the Emporium months ago. She moaned and kicked, struggling to get free, and he shouted, "You want drown right now, girl?"

She stopped struggling, and he began the climb up the rope ladder, Suzannah draped over his shoulder. In the weird shadows cast by the moonlight, it was a fearsome sight, and Daniel closed his eyes.

Down in the longboat, Kio, warned Daniel, "No kicking when I carry . . . or I throw you in water. You hear me?"

Trussed up in the ropes and the tarp, Daniel decided to save his strength. He nodded, and Kio seemed satisfied.

From above, Kao called down to his brother. "Come now!"

Daniel could imagine the headlines of the San Francisco newspapers: *Daniel Colton Kidnapped!* or *Colton Cousins Kidnapped!* Maybe someone would even suspect they had been shanghaied. Not that anyone would ever sail *this* old brig again.

Kio lifted Daniel over his shoulder, and they started up the rope ladder. As the huge man climbed higher and higher, Daniel could see the dim campfires of San Francisco in the distance and the moonlit longboat below. The longboat seemed their only hope of escape. But how—

Before he could come up with a plan, Kio dumped him on the ship's slanting main deck.

"Mmmmmm!" Daniel pleaded in one last attempt.

Kio and Kao stared angrily at him, then started for the rope ladder.

Daniel's heart sank as the two men's heads disappeared behind the railing. After a while, the brig tipped slightly as they climbed off into the longboat. Next came the sound of oars slicing the water as they rowed away. Finally, there was only the creaking of the old brig. And Daniel and Suzannah were alone in the middle of San Francisco Bay.

CHAPTER 10

"Ummmmm . . . ummmmmph!" As Daniel watched in the bright moonlight, Suzannah worked the gag from her mouth.

"Whew! That's a relief!" she said, shaking her head until the gag settled around her neck and long braids. "They must not have tied my gag as tight as yours. I didn't dare work on it while they were still here though. Here . . . let's see if I can try my teeth on yours."

Daniel's spirits lifted as she scooted over on the deck in her canvas tarp. "Turn around."

He turned on his side, and after she was situated behind him, he felt her gnawing at the knot. He'd be glad to get the gag off, but he still didn't know how they were going to get rid of the thick ropes around their wrists and ankles. Worse, the night was growing darker as a bank of stormy clouds rolled over the moon.

"Hold still," she ordered. "When your gag is off, we can yell for help at the top of our lungs."

Little good that would do, Daniel guessed. A few captains had stayed with their ships, of course, but Charles had planned this watery grave well. Most of the ships right around here were truly abandoned and already well on their way to the bottom of the sea. No one would hear their yelling. To make matters worse yet, drops of rain were beginning to patter down, bouncing off the open deck.

By the time Suzannah had eased the knot enough so he could work the gag loose, rain was pouring from the sky. "Thanks, Suz—"

Before he could stop her, she was shouting with all of her might: "H-E-L-P! S-O-M-E-B-O-D-Y, H-E-L-P!"

In spite of his doubts, Daniel heard himself joining in: "H-E-L-P! H-E-R-E! I-N A-N O-L-D B-R-I-G! H-E-L-P!"

They called out over and over, still hopeful. But after a while, their shouts, hurled against the lashing rain and the rising wind, seemed useless.

"We'll have to wait until the rain stops," Daniel decided, squinting through the downpour to get his bearings. "Let's try to get over to the quarterdeck and get out of some of this rain." Slowly, they sat up and slid down the slippery deck, their canvas tarps catching on the rough wood as they moved.

"Why did Charles do this?" Suzannah asked when they had reached the scant shelter of the quarterdeck. "You started to tell me at home in the courtyard when we were so rudely interrupted."

"Because I had just told him I wouldn't work for him anymore."

Suzannah looked startled. "You mean you sold him more goods after that first time?"

"I had to. They stopped me that night I was so late coming home, and he threatened all of you if I didn't give in. Finally I couldn't take it any longer, and this afternoon I told him I was quitting. I think he wanted to scare me into coming back by kidnapping us, but then we heard the gunfire behind his office and . . . well, someone got hit."

Suzannah grew sober. "I heard it too. Do you think Charles is . . . dead?"

Daniel shrugged. "Maybe . . . from what was said. If he is, nobody but Kao and Kio know where we are."

"Maybe they'll change their minds and come back for us . . ." Suzannah's voice trailed off as she realized how unlikely that would be.

"Charles always claimed they'd be loyal to the end. Once their minds were set on following his orders, it's almost as if they couldn't change course."

There was a long pause while Daniel and Suzannah pondered their dilemma. Then Suzannah spoke up, "So what do we do next?"

"The first thing is to get loose somehow."

"Just what I've been trying to do for the last hour!" she complained, still straining against the ropes.

"I'm certain now that Kao and Kio are the ones who robbed the Emporium that first day," Daniel said. "I'll bet that's how Charles got enough money to buy his gambling tent. When we wouldn't give him the money, he had Kao and Kio come to the ship and steal it."

"That would be just like Charles Herrington!" Suzannah answered.

Exhausted from their struggles, they finally lay against the quarterdeck wall. Daniel's hands were so wet that he could feel them slipping a little beneath the ropes. "Hey, maybe the rain will help us, after all!" he said, twisting his wrists this way and that once more.

"It hurts though," Suzannah griped.

Daniel's wrists felt raw, and he was sure they were bleeding. But he kept trying. At long last, he was able to work one hand loose, then pull out the other. "I made it!" He pushed down the canvas tarp so he could wriggle over to Suzannah. When he reached her, he began untying the ropes around her wrists.

After that, it was still hard work to remove the ropes around their legs and ankles. They struggled for a long time until finally Suzannah exclaimed with a whoop of delight, "I'm free! I'm free!" just as Daniel pulled his feet from the coil of rope.

"Now, let's hope we don't sink before we can get off this old brig!" Suzannah said, rubbing her wrists and ankles. "Why don't we explore the ship and see if we can find something we can use to get away?"

Daniel shook his head. "It's too dark, and we don't know the layout of this ship. We'd better stay right here until daylight. Then we'll think of a plan. Now we'd better get some sleep."

"Sleep . . . in this rain?"

"It's dark out, if you hadn't noticed. Can't even see the shoreline now. So we might as well rest up until we can see where we're going."

"All right," she agreed reluctantly. "Just until daylight though."

Huddling together in the corner of the quarterdeck, the two closed their eyes. Visions of their terrifying experience still crowded Daniel's brain, and the old brig creaked and shuddered as if she'd go down any minute.

We've got to get off this ship, Daniel thought to himself, feeling a lot older than his thirteen years and mightily responsible for Suzannah. *But even though we're free of the ropes, it doesn't mean we'll ever make it back. Please, Lord, show us what to do!*

As he lay there, trying not to let Suzannah know how scared he was, bits and pieces of the past rolled through his mind. He thought of his life back home in Virginia . . . the beginning of their long journey West along the National Road . . . riding a stagecoach through a snowstorm . . . the bear chase . . . the encounter with a strange French trapper. Then there had been the covered wagon trek . . . Ned Taylor nearly drowning at the Kansas River crossing . . . wild Indians on the prairies . . . the buffalo stampede when the wagon turned over . . . the unending desert . . . the blizzard in the Rockies. With God's help, he and Suzannah had already lived through more than most folks far older, Daniel decided. Getting them off this abandoned ship shouldn't be too hard for the Lord.

"Are you asleep?" Suzannah asked. She gave him a jab in the ribs. "I'm freezing! We can't stay here. Maybe we could go down on the 'tween deck or the captain's cabin, out of the wind and rain."

"Without a lantern?" Daniel asked, shivering.

"Maybe we'll find one down below. We could pray about it . . . in fact, I'm surprised you haven't thought of that before."

"What makes you think I haven't?" Daniel was ashamed he hadn't prayed out loud with Suzannah, but it was never too late to start. "Let's ask Him to help us find a way out of here."

In all his life, Daniel had never been more sincere. "Lord, Thou hast delivered us from every kind of danger—from storms and blizzards, from wild animals and Indians, from sickness and starvation. We trust Thee now to deliver us from the sea. Show us the way."

"And, Lord," Suzannah added, "Thou hast told us that two are better than one, so we're really glad we have each other. Thou hast said where two or more are gathered in Thy name, Thou art in the midst and will answer our prayers. Well, here we are—two of Thy children—Daniel and Suzannah Colton. We'd like to go home . . . please—" Suzannah's voice wavered and Daniel grabbed her hand.

"Don't worry. He'll help us. Come on! Let's see if we can find that lantern."

Together they crawled across the deck toward the spot where Daniel expected the ship's staircase to be, that is, if it were anything like the other ships he'd visited.

Feeling along the deck, his fingers touched a thick slab of wood. He ran his hand over it, finding a handle on top, and he swallowed hard. "The hatch cover. That means the cargo hole is open. We don't dare fall in."

The rain had let up for a moment, and the moon came out from behind the dark clouds. Now he could clearly make out the hatch cover, and the nearby black hole leading to the insides of the ship.

"There's the staircase!" He stood up and made his way across the slanted deck, still holding Suzannah's hand to steady her. "Careful now . . . careful."

Releasing her hand, he reached for the stairway railing, then tested the step in front of him with his foot. It seemed to be firm, not rotten, as he had feared. He tried another. "So far, so good," he encouraged her.

Moving cautiously, Suzannah started down after him. The old brig tossed with the waves, creaking and groaning with every step they took. Slowly, step by step, they descended the stairway, pausing at the bottom of the steps to let their eyes adjust to the deep darkness.

"This must be the 'tween deck," Daniel said. "If this ship is like the *Bostonia*, the cabins should be forward. Take my hand."

Feeling the walls as he went along, Daniel turned into a passageway.

Suzannah's voice shook. "Let's hope the floor isn't rotten. We'd fall right in."

Suddenly something scurried along under them, running over their feet. "A rat!" Daniel said.

Gripping his hand tightly, Suzannah shuddered. "Ugh! I hate rats!"

"He won't hurt you. Come on." Daniel ran his hand along the wall, then found an indentation. "Wait! Here's a doorway . . . maybe a cabin."

Feeling for a doorknob, he turned it. To his amazement, it was not locked, but creaked open. "Stand back," he told Suzannah. "I'll go in first."

Very slowly, Daniel made his way around the damp walls in the darkness. "A bunk," he reported, moving his hands over the rough wood.

"Anyone in it?" Suzannah teased, with a hint of her old spirit.

Quite suddenly, he imagined a skeleton lying in the bed, and he jumped, feeling a prickle of fear running up his spine. Glad Suzannah had not been able to see him in the dark, he said matter-of-factly, "Nobody. It's empty."

He moved on, feeling his way along. "If we're lucky, there should be a lantern somewhere nearby . . . that is, unless these fellows jumped ship at night and took their lamps with them." Up and down the damp wall he felt, moving slowly, until he bumped into something hard. "Here it is!" he called back to Suzannah, relief in his voice.

"Whatever you do, don't break it!" Suzannah warned.

Daniel paused to brace his feet as the ship rolled forward on a sudden swell. "If only this old brig didn't tilt about so much." He began to unhook the lantern, but once more there was a shift in his position, tearing the hook from the wall. It was all he could do to hold on to the lantern.

"Are there any matches?" Suzannah asked, sounding worried. "There should be some somewhere."

"Here, in the box below . . . matches!"

"Thank goodness!" Suzannah said. "Hurry up and light the lantern. I feel like hundreds of rats are creeping all around us."

Daniel's hands shook. "I'm doing my best." Carefully he sat down on the floor of the cabin, setting the lantern in front of him. "Now, to strike the match." The soles of his shoes were too wet, so he tried rubbing the tip against the wall. Nothing happened. He tried again, then again. "It's too damp." Once more he tried, and the match flared to life.

"Thank you, Lord!" Suzannah breathed.

Daniel's hand was shaking, but finally the lantern was lit and the wick adjusted until it gave off a steady glow. "I've never been so glad to see light," he admitted. He glanced around. No rats. No skeleton in the bunk either. "Looks like an officer's cabin."

With her wet hair plastered around her face, Suzannah's blue-green eyes seemed huge in the lantern light. "Well, we won't find anything here. What we need is a dinghy or a longboat."

Daniel noticed that her clothes, like his, were still soaked from the storm. "What we need is something to keep us warm," he said. "Look . . . there are blankets on those bunks. Let's wrap up in them. Then let's go up on the main deck and see what's what."

Draping the blankets about themselves, Indian-style, Daniel and Suzannah left the cabin and retraced their steps through the passageway. With the lantern held high, it was much easier to make their way up the stairs, even though the ship rolled beneath their feet, groaning in protest against each wave.

When they reached the main deck, the rain was slashing down again, reflecting the lantern glow like thousands of sparkling beads. They bent their head against the downpour and headed for the ship's outer rail. Then clinging to it, they circled the deck in search of a dinghy or longboat.

"Nothing here," Daniel said at last. "I doubt there's anything in the hold either."

"But we have to look," Suzannah insisted.

Daniel nodded. "All right, let's go. At least we'll be out of the rain."

The second trip past the 'tween deck and deep into the dark cargo hold went more quickly with the light to guide them. This time, even though Suzannah was expecting the pairs of bright red eyes peering at them from the darkness, she couldn't stifle her scream.

"It's just the rats," Daniel explained. But his hand wasn't quite steady when he shone the lantern around the watery hold. Tops of barrels and crates rose from the water. No sign of boats. "Let's get out of here!"

Suzannah hurried up the tilting stairs, Daniel right behind her. "It's all right," he told her, "the rats aren't after us. The light just disturbed them."

"I thought rats were supposed to *desert* a sinking ship," she complained. On the 'tween deck, she turned again toward the officer's cabin. "Let's sleep in here. It's warmer and we can close the door. I'd feel safer too."

But Daniel disagreed. "We're better off on the main deck. If this brig sinks, we could at least jump off."

Even in the dim light, Daniel could see Suzannah's eyes become as round as saucers. "Remember?" she said in a small voice. "I can't swim."

"I'm sorry, Suzannah," he said, feeling awful. "I just plain forgot."

A new idea leapt to his mind though. When daylight came, he could swim ashore and get help. It would be a hard swim, but he didn't see any other way. He only hoped the ship wouldn't go down before then.

He opened the door to the officer's cabin. "You're right. We'd be warmer sleeping in here."

Suzannah followed and quickly shut the door behind them.

"You can have the bunk," Daniel told her. "I'll sleep on the floor."

Suzannah inspected the bunk and rolled her eyes. "Rat droppings."

Daniel shuddered. "Then we can both sleep on the floor by the lantern. It gives off some warmth."

He settled on one side of the lantern, and she lay down on the other. With the floor tilting this way and that, it was all they could do to keep from sliding about. It took several tries before they discovered how to brace themselves by pushing their feet against the wall.

At long last, Daniel's eyes drifted shut, and he slept.

"Fire, Daniel! Fire!"

Daniel's eyes opened wide. The end of Suzannah's blanket was ablaze . . . and the bunk behind her! The lantern had tipped over and was spilling a trail of flames across the cabin floor.

Jumping to his feet, he snatched the burning blanket away from her, setting his own blanket afire. He tossed it aside, and the flames leapt up the wall.

"Come on!" he yelled, opening the cabin door. Suzannah stood rooted to the floor in terror, and he grabbed her arm. "Hurry! We've got to get out of here!"

Leaving the cabin door open so they could find the stairway, they raced over to it. Tripping over her skirt, Suzannah scooped it up and held it over her arm.

"Hurry!" called Daniel, turning to see what was keeping her. "That fire is spreading!"

They stumbled up the stairway and onto the main deck, the flames flaring after them. The rain had stopped—just when they needed it!

"What'll we do now?" Suzannah cried.

"Pray like anything . . . for a miracle!"

Daniel closed his eyes and prayed with all of his being. "Help, Lord! We don't know what to do!" Even in the confusion, the still, small voice seemed to answer: *Keep on trying . . . keep on . . . keep on.*

When Daniel opened his eyes, the flames were leaping up the stairway. He glanced about, but there was no way of escape except to swim, and he couldn't leave Suzannah behind. "Come on!" he urged. "Help me slide the cargo hatch back on. Maybe we can keep the fire below a while longer."

Suzannah looked doubtful, but she followed him quickly to the hatch. "Maybe someone will see the fire and think it's a signal—"

They tugged at the heavy hatch cover. Suddenly the ship lurched, and the slippery cover slid from their grasp. It bumped down the slanting deck, stopping with a loud crack near the railing. "That's it!" yelled Daniel. "There's our answer! It's a perfect raft!"

"A raft?"

"Sure! We can sit on it, each gripping a handle, and holding a tarp up between us for a sail."

Suzannah glanced back at the fire. The flames had broken through the cargo hold and were racing across the deck. "I guess there's nothing else we can do! I'll help!"

It took a mighty effort to wrestle the wooden hatch cover up over the ship's railing, but finally they succeeded. "There it goes!" Suzannah cried. They watched it fall into the water while the fire roared behind them. "It's landing handles up, too!"

Daniel nodded. "Now to get down the rope ladder," he said. "I'll go first with a tarp. Hurry! But be careful!"

"What if I fall?"

Daniel knew he wouldn't be able to catch her. As it was, he'd only be able to hold onto the rope ladder with one hand while he carried the tarp with the other. "Just don't look down. Take the ladder one rung at a time."

He started down, hanging on with one hand. Halfway to the swirling water below, he saw that the hatch cover had jammed against the burning ship. Good! He looked up.

Silhouetted by the red blaze, Suzannah was leaning over the side, trying not to look down. "Here I come!"

"One step at a time!" he reminded her.

It seemed that they swayed on the rotting rope ladder forever. Finally, Daniel reached the bottom and stepped onto the unsteady cargo cover, balancing until he could sit in the middle. Above him, Suzannah was still climbing down, coming closer and closer in the firelight. "When you get here, try to put your feet in the middle of this hatch cover!" he yelled over the sound of the roaring flames. "Careful . . . careful . . . we don't have much time!"

He paddled the water with his hands to keep their makeshift raft close to the ship. "Slowly now," he directed as she neared the bottom.

As Suzannah stepped onto the hatch cover, it shifted suddenly, moving them away from the ship. "Yiii!" she yelled, slipping.

Daniel grabbed her, and they fell in a tangle of arms and legs on the cover. Holding their breath, they sat up, steadying their makeshift raft. Above them, the old brig burned brightly, lighting the night with an orange glow.

"Paddle away from her!" Daniel yelled. "Use your hands!"

Although they both paddled for all they were worth, they made little progress. And up above, the flaming mast showered sparks on them, and burning timbers fell, sizzling as they hit the water.

"There!" Daniel said, plucking a long piece of wood from the water. The timber was still steaming hot. He ignored the pain as he pushed it against the hull of the brig.

"Hurry!" Suzannah begged, still paddling with her hands.

Daniel pressed them away steadily as the burning ship rained sparks all around. Slowly, very slowly, they moved away from the fiery brig.

Turning, Daniel caught a glimpse of the campfires on the distant shore. "Town's that way!" he said, using the timber to pole their little craft through the jumble of old wrecks. He pushed off against the stern of one ship, then the bow of another, and Suzannah paddled as fast as she could.

Behind them, the old brig lit up the night. With the burning ship behind and the coastal campfires ahead to guide them, they navigated the waters of the bay, still weaving through the graveyard of half-sunken ships. At last they broke away.

Daniel felt weak. "Now we grab a handle with one hand and hold the sail up between us with the other," he told Suzannah.

"There's not much wind," she remarked, helping set the makeshift sail as the first pale rays of sunshine stained the dark sky. After a while, she said, "We're moving a little!"

Faster and faster they sailed toward the campfires on the shore. "It's the tide!" Daniel exclaimed. "The tide's taking us ashore!"

Suzannah blew up her damp bangs. "What if it had been going out to sea? We'd be heading for the middle of the Pacific Ocean by now!"

All of a sudden, Daniel felt like laughing crazily. "What a sight we must make. I feel like the *Bostonia*, sailing in across the bay the day we grounded her."

"You don't look like her at all," Suzannah returned with the famous Colton grin. "*Your* sails are all black!" she said, pointing to the smudges of smoke on his face. Then, catching sight of movement on the beach, she cried, "It looks like

Uncle Franklin and Big Red! They see us! They're waving! Ahoy! Ahoy!"

On shore, Father and Big Red dragged a longboat into the water, jumped in, and began to row. When they were within shouting distance, they called out, "Are you all right?"

"Fine!" Daniel shouted. "We're fine!"

The longboat came alongside the raft, and while Big Red steadied the boat, Father pulled Suzannah and Daniel to him. "Thank God," he said, his arms circling them. "Thank God."

Father loosened his hold on them. "We'd better get you back to Mother and Pauline," he said. "They're worried sick about you."

He and Big Red turned the boat around and headed for shore, their long strokes and the tide helping them to cover the distance in short order. When they reached land and were satisfied that Suzannah and Daniel were unharmed, they bundled them in warm blankets for the wagon ride home.

"I'm proud of you, Son," Father said when he and Big Red turned the horses toward Rancho Encino. "Not only did you prove yourself to be a fine frontiersman on the trail West, but now you're a sailor too."

From their nest in a pile of quilts in the wagon bed, Suzannah laughed, unable to resist giving Daniel a friendly poke in the ribs. "We'll have to call him *Captain* Colton now—Captain of the Cover Hatch! . . . But I have to admit he saved my life."

Daniel grinned. "I can't take all the credit. You helped too. Where would we be now if you hadn't chewed off my gag? But remember . . . there were *three* of us on that ship—"

Father turned from his place in the driver's seat and looked at him in surprise. *"Three?"*

Daniel nodded. "Suzannah, me . . . and the Lord. He's the *real* Captain!"

They rode in silence for a long time, pondering all that had happened in the past few hours.

At last Father broke into their thoughts. "I'm afraid I have some sad news for you," he began, speaking over his shoulder. "Charles . . . is dead."

"We thought so," Daniel replied, suddenly sober. "We heard gunfire, then a man say he'd 'gotten the gambler.' We figured it had to be Charles."

"Is Pauline very upset?" Suzannah wanted to know.

"She's heartbroken, of course," said Father, "but now she can begin to heal. If Charles had lived, he would have broken her heart many more times." There was a long pause. "When did the shooting take place?" he asked, turning to Daniel.

Daniel felt numb. "Just before Charles sent us off with his bodyguards to that abandoned ship—"

"Charles was behind that?" Big Red asked angrily, the veins standing out in his forehead. Daniel had never seen him so mad before. "That was the last thing he did?"

"I suppose so," Daniel replied miserably.

As they traveled home, it occurred to him that evil had won out in Charles's life. But Daniel Colton didn't have to be caught up in it. First he'd have to forgive Charles for everything—even the kidnapping! Next, he'd have to ask his father to forgive *him* for not confiding in him. Hiding his problem had only made things worse for everyone.

Two days later, big drops of rain pattered down on the new family graveyard under a stand of oak trees. The Coltons and the Stenglers stood beneath black umbrellas near the wooden coffin Uncle Karl had built for Charles. Pauline wept, tears rolling down her cheeks like the endless rain.

On her right, Mother patted her arm comfortingly, and on her left, Father was holding Jamie. Suzannah stood off to the side, biting her lip. Daniel knew she was struggling, like him, with a mixture of grief and relief. At the head of the coffin, Big Red waited to say a few words over the body. Everyone looked heartsick, as if they'd all failed God.

What could a preacher say at a time like this? Daniel wondered. Charles had certainly been no fit husband or father or brother-in-law. As for his so-called friends in town, not one of them had come to pay their respects. *Lord, give Big Red wisdom,* Daniel prayed. *Pauline needs comfort.*

Big Red opened the big black Bible and read from the book of Jeremiah about knowing God. The passage ended, "I am the Lord which exercise lovingkindness, judgment, and righteousness, in the earth: for in these things I delight, saith the Lord."

He looked up. "We're not s'posed to judge or condemn," he reminded them. "Judgment belongs to the Lord. Our job is to tell folks the good news about Jesus Christ.

"So today we commit Charles Herrington's body to the earth from which it came. He himself will stand before the great white judgment throne, and we can say most sincerely, 'May God have mercy on his soul.'"

He looked at the family gathered around the grave. "Charles can no longer hear us, but you can. Each one of us standin' here is called on to decide about committin' himself to Jesus Christ as Savior and Lord. It's a matter of life and death. Since nobody knows how long we'll live on this earth, we'd best decide soon. Will we choose the world and death . . . or everlastin' life with Christ?"

There was not a sound except for Pauline's soft crying and the plunking of the raindrops on the wet oak leaves. Suddenly, to Daniel's astonishment, Uncle Karl stepped forward and grabbed Big Red's hand. His Adam's apple bobbed as he said, "I repent . . . and I choose Christ!"

Daniel could not believe his ears, and Pauline moved over to hug Uncle Karl, fresh tears springing to her eyes. "I've prayed so hard that something good might come of this," she said. "If Charles couldn't help anyone while he was living . . ." she swallowed . . . "maybe in death he can be a blessing."

"That's a fact," Uncle Karl said. "While I was hammerin' that coffin together, I saw the error of followin' my own way."

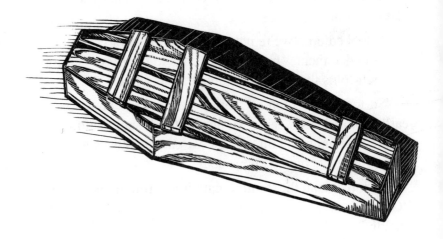

"I had no idea you were considering becoming a Christian, Karl," Mother said.

Daniel just stood, wonderstruck. *God sure had mysterious ways of working things out,* he thought. It reminded him of the first Easter. When all seemed lost, Christ had risen from the grave. And now, just when evil seemed about to triumph, God had used Charles's funeral to bring eternal life to Uncle Karl's soul.

"Praise God!" Aunt Pearl exclaimed. "I've prayed and prayed, Karl . . . that someday our family would be together in the Lord!"

Daniel's thoughts returned to the journey westward. At the fork in the trail, Father had said, "We must keep the family together. Nothing is more important."

At last, Daniel thought, *the journey's over, and the family is really together!*

EPILOGUE

———◆◆◆———

A year later, Daniel stood in his dark blue suit behind Big Red in the sunny parlor. Suzannah, her blue-green eyes the color of her dress, waited behind Pauline. As Aunt Pearl played softly on the organ, Daniel clamped down on his lips to hide a grin. It was amazing to think what had led to this wedding. In one split moment, he remembered.

Some months ago, he and Big Red had carried on a discussion about Pauline and whether she would ever marry again. For no reason at all, Daniel had asked, "Why don't *you* ask her?"

Big Red's eyes had widened with hope, then he shook his head. "Aw, she's much too fine a lady to marry *me*."

"I think she likes you anyway," Daniel had persisted. "I think she likes you a lot—"

"But I ain't had much schoolin', and I don't always talk right," Big Red protested. "Miss Pauline's been brought up for finer things."

Daniel shook his head. "Charles was handsome and he could talk real good, but you're finer than he ever was. You're gentle and kind, and you love the Lord. Besides, I think you love her and the children too."

"Reckon I do—" He stopped, shaken by what he had said. "Do . . . do you think she'd have me for a husband?"

Daniel could scarcely believe that Big Red would even discuss such a grown-up matter with him. "Why don't you ask her?"

Today they stood in the sunny parlor with a real minister to lead the marrying vows. Daniel listened to every word, in case he was ever called to preach. Now the time had come to hand Big Red the gold ring. Daniel gave it to him and watched him put it on Pauline's finger.

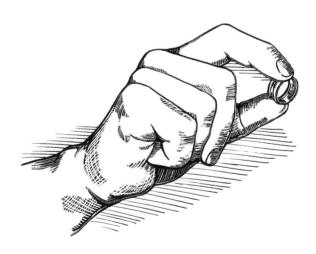

The minister proclaimed for all to hear, "I now pronounce you man and wife. You may kiss the bride."

As the wedding couple's eyes met with joy and love, Daniel felt his face grow bright red. He slid his eyes sideways and they lit on Suzannah. Not surprisingly, she was biting down on her lips to keep from laughing at his embarrassment.

He clamped his own mouth tight. *Just wait till this wedding is over, Suzannah Colton!* he thought. *I'll get you . . . I'll get you yet!* Suddenly he realized that she was wearing her hair up on top of her head for the wedding . . . now when—for the first time in ages—he felt like tugging her braids and running like anything.